ROMANIA

HAWKS MC NEXT GENERATION

USA TODAY BESTSELLING AUTHOR

LILA ROSE

1st Print Edition
ISBN: 978-1-7635597-8-3

*This dedication was written by my daughter, Shayla.
I'd stepped away from writing Rommy and came back to find
the words below:*

To my wonderful daughter also my favourite child. Jake sucks.

AUTHOR'S NOTE:

Please be aware that since this story is mainly from Romania's POV, the spelling will be in Australian English. Colloquial US slang and phrasing has been used for American characters so characters stay true to their voices and their setting.

Please email me if you have any concerns about mistakes: lilarose2678@gmail.com.

<u>For example:</u>

USA say: Ass
AUS say: Arse
USA say: Mom
AUS say: Mum

CHAPTER ONE

ROMANIA

Walking into the break room in the mechanics garage, I called, "Hey, hi, hello, guys." I loved saying all three together. One was never enough, and all three made things cheerier, especially here at work. I hoped my greeting made people happier. Plus the biker brothers around me seemed to smile when they heard me say it.

I headed straight for the table and the chocolate muffins. I picked one up as I got side hugged.

Glancing up, I gave Dive a chocolate-mouth smile, which had him laughing. "How goes it, Rommy?"

I loved being called Rommy instead of Romania. My full name always made me think I was getting into trouble.

After swallowing, I said, "Good, good. How's things with you? Is Mena coming in today? How's Koda with school? You know, when I was seventeen, I started to look at boys in a new light. Have you given Koda the sex talk yet?"

Dive blinked down at me. I tended to have that type of reaction from people because I said what came to mind. And honestly, there tended to be a lot buzzing around in my head. But also, I sometimes never thought about my words before blurting them out.

Thankfully, the brothers knew how to take me. It helped that I'd grown up around this mob since I was seven.

Dive grinned. "The talk has been had. No problem there. And Mena is making lunch for the club today, so she'll be here later."

"Wicked. I love her cooking," I said around a mouthful of muffin.

He-he, that's so not the first muffin I've had near my mouth.

Dive winked, leaning in to kiss my temple before saying, "Gonna grab a mug of coffee. You want?"

When I shook my head, still munching on my treat, he slipped over to the coffee counter.

Dive was my dad's closest brother and friend. He's more like an uncle to me and my brother, Texas. Growing up, we spent a lot more of our time around Dive, Mena, and Koda than the rest of the brothers.

Still, the club was like one big family anyway, which I loved.

My life was damn blessed. I loved the people around me, where I worked, my bike, and the books I read. I still lived at home, but I wasn't looking at wasting my money on a billion bills when I didn't have to. I wanted to travel and have fun for a couple of years before I decided to do adulting stuff.

I just had to convince Mum and Dad to trust that I'd be safe travelling on my own. I wanted to go from one place to another whenever I wished, to do what I wanted without anyone breathing down my neck.

I'd saved enough money again after I purchased my own ride and put funds into making her the perfect bike for me.

Now I wanted to see the world.

"Rommy," Dad called, holding up a bottle of strawberry milk. When I nodded, he threw it my way. Lucky I was good at catching.

"Thanks, Dad," I called, chocolate pieces flying out of my mouth. *Oops.*

"Keep it in your mouth," he said with a sigh.

After swallowing, I voiced, "That's what he said."

I grinned, getting a few chuckles though mostly groans around me.

Dad shook his head. "Get to work," he ordered.

I saluted him with my drink and walked out into the garage. As I passed Knife and Beast, who were working on a 1970 Holden Ute, I whistled. "That's gonna purr like a kitten when you two are done."

Knife smirked. "She won't be the only one I make purr."

Knife chuckled when Beast shoved him and signed, *"Who the fuck are you talking about?"*

"You, babe," Knife said, making sure Beast could read his lips. "Always you." He leaned in for a quick kiss.

They were adorable.

Not that I'd tell them that. But I loved love. Seeing it, hearing about it, feeling it, and reading about it.

Love was such a strong emotion. It could be beautiful but painful at times too.

I wanted what so many couples around me had—a love that could survive every trial and come out stronger on the other side.

"Later, guys," I called to Knife and Beast with a wave before I made my way over to my workstation and the silver Nissan Pulsar—a customer's speedway car I was working on. Bikes were my usual go-to, but I liked cars just as much.

Fun cars. Cars that made my motor run in an excited way.

As soon as I slipped on my coveralls and turned on my music through my headphones, I became lost in my world as I worked.

Music helped me from overthinking since my mind fired off so many thoughts per second. A teacher had asked Mum and Dad to have me tested for autism and ADHD, and since they were the best people in my life, they talked to me about it first to see if I wanted to be tested.

I already knew I was different. My family did, too, of course. I mean they were around me all the time. But I didn't want to put a label to my—as Mum called it— "uniqueness."

If people couldn't take me as I was, then they weren't worth knowing.

There'd been many people I learned that lesson from. A lot who only put up with me to get to my brother or the Hawks motorcycle club.

But I also had many who had my back. Who loved me.

And one day I'd find my true love. If it was with a man or a woman, I wouldn't know until that time came.

A couple of hours later, I was tightening the final screw

when I sensed someone in my area. Looking up, I smiled and removed my headphones.

"Billy, what's up?"

"Got a client wantin' to book in with you for a service later in the week."

I screwed up my nose. "Prospects take care of those jobs."

"I know. This guy saw you in the article in the newspaper and wants to pay a shitload more than usual for a service." The local newspaper had wanted to do a piece on the garage because we'd donated a heap of money to the local cancer centre. They interviewed a few employees to talk about the garage, and I'd been one of them. Even had my photo taken too.

Snorting, I said, "I ain't servicing his pecker if that's what he thinks."

Billy choked on an abrupt laugh. "Yeah, look, I wasn't sure about even bringin' this to you. But I also didn't know if you want the extra cash to do an easy job."

I shrugged. "Sure, why not."

He nodded. "Don't worry, Rommy, we'll keep an eye on him."

Grinning, I winked. "I know you guys will." I picked up a rag and started cleaning my hands. "While you're in the office, if Mum's not in there, can you call the Nissan owner and tell him she's ready?"

He tipped his chin up. "You got it," he said before walking away.

I went to the driver's side of the car and made sure the cover on the seat was in place before I put my grubby coveralls on the material. Once seated, I turned the key, and when the engine roared to life, it was like an orgasm without penetration.

A few of the brothers looked over, grinning.

I drove her from my spot in the garage and parked her in front of the shop before climbing out and removing the plastic sheet from the seat. I pocketed the keys and went straight into the office. Billy wasn't around, but someone else was.

"Girl, you've done a good job. She sounds sweet."

"Thanks, Mum. Did you or Billy call the owner?"

Mum smirked. "I found Billy on the phone when I came in, and he told me that the owner checked if you would be around when he came to pick it up in an hour."

There was a creak of a chair in the office behind Mum.

Mum winced and muttered, "I shouldn't've opened his door."

Dad stopped in the doorway. "Who was askin' this? What's the guy's name?" Dad moved over to the counter where the invoices were laid out.

"Dad," I whined. "You understand I'm a twenty-three-year-old woman with needs." I kept a straight face, enjoying teasing him.

Mum looked away, but I saw her shoulders shaking when Dad coughed and spluttered and turned red.

"Kid. Fucking hell. I don't need to know anythin'. You go to your mum about that shit and just tell me if or when I need to hurt someone."

"Okay." I grinned.

He sighed, turned, and walked back into his office.

"You're evil," Mum whispered.

"But it was funny, right?"

She pinched her forefinger and thumb together. "Go get a snack, and I'll let you know when the GSX-R arrives."

I blew her a kiss. "You're the best," I said before leaving. This time, instead of the break room connected to the garage, I went into the compound.

On the way to the kitchen, I greeted brothers and their women, some kids too. But all I could think about was getting my hands on one of those monster cookies that I saw yesterday.

The brothers had better have left one for me or there'd be hell to pay.

I had a deep relationship with food. Food loved me, and I loved it. I'd give anything a try at least once, and so far, the only thing I had tried and didn't like was when Texas had dared me to eat frog's legs that time we'd gone to a fancy restaurant to celebrate Mum and Dad's anniversary.

A restaurant we'd never step foot in again since my stomach had revolted at putting frog's legs in it, and I ended up spraying their bathroom with vomit.

Now it was funny, but back then, I wanted to die of mortification.

Huh, I like that word.

Mortification.

I wanted to use it more often.

Pushing through the doors, I said, "Mena, hey, hi, hello." I walked up behind her to hug around the waist to avoid the marinade all over her hands.

"Hi, Rommy. How's your morning been?"

"Amazing. I just finished a car, and I have a bike coming in soon." I didn't bother telling Mena about what was wrong with the car or what type. I noticed a lot of the women in my life really didn't care to hear about vehicles. "Have you seen any of those big cookies around? Oh, and what are we having for lunch? Are the club girls helping you? You should have more help in here." I glanced through some plastic containers as I talked.

The club girls were women who stayed in the compound for free and in return they got to party hard and sex it up with the single brothers. But Mum made sure they pulled their weight with cleaning and cooking too.

"The cookies are on the left up the top. Knife tried to hide them yesterday. Don't tell him I said that."

Laughing, I shook my head. "My lips are sealed." I took the container down and opened the lid, moaning at the sight of the chocolate-chip goodness. I grabbed one out and placed the container back before facing Mena again.

"For lunch, I'm making some pastries as well as meat skewers and salads. Dinner, I'm preparing the chicken." She nodded down at the big bowl she had her hands stuffed in. "The club girls will finish off dinner, but I told them I didn't need help for lunch." She smiled.

"I'm already looking forward to lunch," I told her.

She huffed. "When aren't you looking forward to food?"

"Ha, true." My cell chimed with a text. It was Mum telling me the bike was here. I shoved the rest of the cookie in my mouth and waved to Mena. "Got to go," I told her and winced when bits of cookie flew out.

Mena laughed. "Get out of here."

With another wave, I made my way back into the garage.

"Rommy, a prospect is bringing the bike into your bay now," Billy said.

"Thanks." By the time I reached my area, the GSX-R

1000 was already parked and waiting for me. She was a red beauty, and I couldn't wait to work on her. The customer complained of a rattle when running, and it was up to me to figure out what the problem was and fix it. Smiling, I redressed into my coveralls and reached for my headphones to place them on. I selected a playlist and got busy.

Sometime later, I felt a tap on my shoulder and slightly jolted. It was lucky—for that person—I trusted everyone around me, or else I would have flipped them over my shoulder for startling me.

Pulling my headphones off, I looked to Fang. He tipped his chin up and said, "The customer for the car you worked on is here askin' for you."

Grinning, I blew him a kiss. "Thanks, Fang." As I started to wipe down my hands, I asked, "How's the family?"

His smile grew. "Perfect."

"Awesome. Tell Poppy she has to come to the next girls' night."

"I will. She's pissed she had a cold and missed the last one when Swan was here."

"I'll make sure the Ballarat girls come back up for another one. It'll be epic." We walked towards the office talking, and then Fang split off to head out into the compound.

Entering the office, I noticed Peter, the customer, was already looking at me. Glancing to Mum, I saw she was pretending to be busy with something on the computer.

"Peter, your baby is all ready for the race on the weekend."

He smiled, stepping my way. "I knew it would be since you're the one working on it."

"There was nothing really to report, and I see you have the keys. Did you fix the bill with M—"

"He sure did," Mum said quickly. Like she didn't want me to call her Mum in front of him. But why?

"Cool. Is there anything else I can help with?" I asked. Would he ask me out?

"Actually...."

A giddy flutter started in my belly. He was going to ask, and I was happy to go on a date with him since he was cute and sweet.

A chair creaked behind me just as the office door opened and in filed Dive, Knife, Beast, Billy, and Pick. Billy, at least, looked like he didn't want to be there. And I absolutely knew Dad had texted them.

"Are we having a meeting I didn't know about?" I asked. Frustration had my tone more snappish than normal, but I couldn't blame the guys or my dad when they were doing this to protect me.

Still, it was annoying; they knew I was a machine in my own right.

Hell, I knew how to throat punch a guy while stabbing his eye at the same time.

Facing Peter, I told him, "Ignore the idiots. What were you going to say?"

The poor guy was too busy taking in the rough-and-tough men around me, who were wearing their club cuts, which he was also checking out.

Goddamn it. I already knew this guy wouldn't ask me out before he stuttered, "N-Nothing. Thanks for your work, Rommy," he said and then quickly fled.

When I turned to the brothers, who were trying to file

back out of the office, I barked, "Stop right there." When they actually froze, my eyes widened. "I know Dad put you all up to this because he doesn't like the thought of me growing up. But, fellas, you will all suffer the consequences along with my father at lunch where I'll be informing you all about a menstrual cycle."

Dad shifted. "Now, Rommy. We're—"

Rolling my eyes, I quickly finished what he would say, "Just looking out for me. I know. But please, *please*, remember that I'm more than capable of taking care of myself. As soon as he nearly peed himself seeing you lot, I knew he wasn't for me, so I do appreciate that, but let me figure these things out on my own, or I'm going to start making all your lives hell. Hear me?"

The brothers grumbled and nodded before they left, and I turned to Dad.

He smirked. "I'll try, okay?"

Smiling, I nodded. "That's all I'm asking." I walked up to him and went to my toes to kiss his cheek. "This still doesn't get anyone out of my talk at lunch." Turning, I called, "Bye, Mum."

"Later, girl," she replied with humour in her tone.

One day soon, they'd see I wasn't a little girl who needed their overprotectiveness.

No, I wasn't the sharpest tool in the shed, but I wasn't stupid either. I could tell who was a douche a mile away. And if the guy or gal hid their douchiness, well, I'd eventually figure them out in the end.

But it was up to me to learn from my mistakes.

CHAPTER TWO

*L*ater in the week, as I walked back into the garage from the compound waiting for the guy who wanted his car serviced, my phone rang. I pulled it out of my back pocket and hit Answer.

"Yo, bro, what's shaking?"

"You're lucky I'm even talkin' to you."

Laughing, I asked, "Are you still butthurt I didn't get my first tattoo from you?"

"Who's your blood brother?" Texas demanded.

"You. But you weren't in town and Dragon was. I promise, the next one I get I'll come to you in Ballarat for it."

"You fuckin' better. The reason I rang was to see if you wanted to come stay next weekend."

"Aww, is my bro missing me?" I teased. Texas and I had always been close, and I was over-the-freaking-moon happy that we'd stayed that way even when he moved an hour away to live with the love of his life, Maya.

"Like a hole in the head," Texas deadpanned, but I knew he was messing with me.

"Can you do another tattoo that weekend? I've always wanted a phoenix. It'll look so cool on my thigh. What do you think?"

"We could make it work. Dodge and Low are comin' too." Texas never chose to call Dodge and Low Mum and Dad like I did. He was just that bit older than me when they took us in.

"Yay, family time with everyone. Maya will be home, right? I want to know all the gossip." I gasped. "We should invite Julian over too. He knows everything about everyone."

Texas sighed. "I'll see, okay?"

"Wait, is Maya pregnant? Did you hear Channa is? I can't wait until Channa has her baby. How do you think Coyote will handle the birth?" I laughed at the thought. These bikers were tough, but when it came to their partners being in pain, they didn't do well. "Hang on, back to Maya. Is she pregnant? Oh my God, imagine if she is and it's at the same time as Channa. That would be so cool. So, is she?" When he didn't reply right away, I pressed, "Texas?"

"Jesus, Rom. Just come to Ballarat, yeah?" When he hung up, I gasped and stared down at my phone.

She's pregnant, for sure.

That he didn't say anything told me everything.

Maya was going to have a little baby.

Holy shit, I'm going to be an aunty.

I did a little happy dance.

"What are you doin', kiddo?"

I squealed and spun to see Dad grinning like an idiot for scaring me.

Shit. I couldn't say anything. I was sure I was right, but in case I wasn't, I had to keep my lips sealed. Also, I was sure Texas and Maya wanted to tell Mum and Dad instead of hearing the news from me.

"Nothing," I yelled.

His grin disappeared and his brows pinched. "Romania."

Goddamn it. He full named me.

I was in trouble.

I had to lie.

"I was just, ah, sexting." That should stop him from questioning anything.

He opened his mouth, closed it, and turned to march the other way.

Grinning, I pumped the air with my fist. All I ever had to do was talk about my period or sex and the guys would stop annoying or questioning me. Giggling, I thought of the other day when I did give the brothers a speech at lunch about women bleeding from our vaginas. There were a large number who paled, and I was sure Knife even heaved a little.

Good times. Good times.

"Rommy, there's a customer here, and Low's not at the desk," a prospect called.

"I got it," I told him, making my way to the office. It was probably for me anyway. As soon as I entered, my belly twisted with the heebie-jeebies from the guy looking my way. Maybe it was the greasy hair or the unkempt look or the way his gaze slowly ran up and down my body.

I stopped just inside the door. "Hi. How can I help you?"

"Romania Monroe, it's a *pleasure*. I have my car booked in with you for a service." His smile even put me off.

"Sure, no problem. Just leave the keys—"

"No."

I jerked my head back. "What? Look, man, if you're going to be a problem, you can get out of here or I'll call in all the other employees to help you leave." I wouldn't mind kicking his ass too, but I didn't want to touch him.

He smirked. "Sorry, I mean I'd prefer to give you the keys." He reached into his pocket and pulled the set out, holding them my way in his gloved hand.

My skin itched at the thought of getting close.

I wanted to punch myself in the tit for accepting this job.

Never again would I think of money first.

Clenching my teeth, I moved closer and stretched my arm out. He dropped the keys into my palm and nodded towards the exit.

"Are you able to come out so I can ask about something on the car? I'm worried it's not safe for my daughter, but she tells me I'm just being silly."

Damn. This guy had a daughter he just wanted safe. I felt like a turd for judging him on the way he looked. There was a chance he didn't have time for a shower that morning. It *was* early.

"Sure." I nodded.

He dipped his head down. "Thank you."

"After you," I said and waited for him to move first. I followed slowly towards the white van.

A white van? Why would he give his daughter a white van?

I stilled.

Was there movement in the back?

Alarm bells went off in my mind.

As I took a step back, the man turned and smiled. "Please, it's just the right-side wheel." He stepped closer to me.

Run, run, run.

Before I could turn, his hand lifted, and he blew something in my face. I started choking and coughing, my eyes stinging. Doors opened, and hands grabbed me. I screamed and blindly kicked and punched.

I let out another scream and then heard, "Hey, leave her the fuck alone." Dad was there.

A cloth slapped over my mouth and nose, a car started, and I was lifted, still struggling.

I heard Dad's sharp "Hawks!" before I was shoved into the van. "Rommy!" Dad roared.

I wanted to yell, to call out, but I was losing the fight, slowly fading.

"Go—"

"What about you?"

"Just go."

A door shut, and the last thought I had before passing out was how pissed Dad was going to be.

DODGE

"No!" I roared, my feet pounding gravel as I ran across the car park to get my girl out of that fucking van. Brothers surrounded me, all fighting to get there in time.

The door to the van slammed shut, and my gut dropped as it took off.

"Fuck," I screamed. "Follow," I ordered, panic clear in my sharp tone.

They'd left one behind. He was headed for another car.

"Dodge, you get to Low. Let us handle it," Dive suggested, throwing a hand towards Low's car coming in.

Fuck. Fuck!

I kept running for the cunt left behind. He'd have the answers I'd need. Other brothers sped out on their rides after the van.

Pick closed in on the guy at the car. The fucker turned, door open, Taser in hand. Before I could shout a warning, he fired at Pick, who shook and went down.

The guy slipped into the car just as Dive and I reached him. I punched through his window, grabbing at him. He started driving, and I ran to keep up, but each time I had a hold of him, he got loose.

"Dodge, let go," Dive shouted.

I made one last effort, but the car was going too fucking fast. I fell to the ground.

"We're on him," Knife called from his bike. He and Beast sped out of the parking lot to follow him.

I dropped to my back, staring up at the sky, tears clouding my vision.

Failed.

I'd fucking failed at protecting my girl.

Darkness clouded my vision, and I roared up at the damned sky, my chest shattering open and leaving me hollow.

"Trey?" I hadn't heard the fear in Low's voice for so fucking long.

Locking my shit down, I stumbled to my feet as Low stopped in front of me. She gripped my tee and shook her head, tears welling, bottom lip trembling. "Tell me it ain't true. Tell me, Trey. Tell me!"

"I couldn't stop them, little bird." An invisible fist punched me in the chest. "They got her."

"No." She shook her head before pushing her face against my chest and breaking. Her sob had my throat thickening. I held her to me.

We'll get her back. I promise. And anyone who's fucking touched her will pay in pain.

But I couldn't get the words out.

Fuck.

Fucking hell.

I wrapped Low up in my arms. "We'll get her back," I managed, jaw clenching. Drawing in a deep breath, I once again locked my emotions down. Over her shoulder, I ordered. "Dive, ring Talon. I want everyone here."

"You got it," my brother said.

As I heard Dive on the phone, I pulled Low back and swiped at her cheeks. I clenched my jaw again at the anguish in her gaze.

My beautiful woman went to her toes and cupped my cheeks, kissing me lightly. "She'll be fine." She was trying to reassure me. I nodded. "We prepared her well for this type of shit."

"We did." Our girl could handle herself. She knew how to fight. She knew how to handle a weapon. But even knowing all that wouldn't clear the fear slamming into me over and over. "She'll be okay," I said.

Low's gaze welled again. "She will."

A throat cleared, and I looked to Dive. "Talon and the brothers are comin'. They're bringin' Texas."

I nodded and curled Low under my arm as she wound both of hers around my waist. "I need to be near the phones in case one of the brothers calls."

She nodded. "Let's get inside then."

"The women will be here soon too."

Low whimpered. Yeah, she'd need her friends' support like I had my brothers'.

Together, we'd handle this. Together, we'd find those fucking motherfuckers and destroy them.

CHAPTER THREE

ROMANIA

My heart thumped hard when I woke in a dark space. I slowly sat up, which made my head spin a little.

"Careful," someone said and then I felt a hand on my arm.

I gripped it, bending the fingers back.

"Shit. Stop. Please stop. I'm just trying to help." The panic and fear in his voice was enough to get me to stop.

Dropping my hold, I cleared my throat to say, "Sorry."

He huffed. "It's okay. Bound to happen when waking up in the dark after being drugged. My name is Cal Berry. In here also is Jenny and Iola."

They both gave me a quiet greeting.

"I'm Romania, but call me Rommy. Do you know

where we are? How many are holding us and why they took us?"

Someone shifted around before Cal said, "Wouldn't have a clue. I think there were three men who grabbed me. Jenny?"

"Three," she answered.

"Iola?" Cal asked.

"Three," she whispered. "Was it the same for you, Rommy?"

"One approached me, but there were more in the van. I couldn't tell how many, though." Blindly reaching out, I started to feel around me. Besides the company I had, there was nothing but steel. "We must be in some type of large container."

"Or a coffin," Cal said.

I shook my head. "It's way too big for that." I stood and found a wall. I wanted to guide myself around the area to see how much space we had, but before I did, I instructed, "Lift your fingers and tuck yourself in so I don't step on you."

"What are you doing?" Jenny asked. Her tone was deeper to Iola's, so it was easy to differentiate.

"Checking what's around us and to see if I can hear anything." I pressed my ear to the wall I had my hands up against.

"I never even thought to do that. Do you hear anything?" Cal asked.

"Nothing yet." I moved down and stopped to listen again. I did the same for all sides of the container. Either the steel had good insulation that kept all sounds out or nothing was happening outside close by.

I sat back down. "I can't hear anything. You're all from Melbourne, right?"

They agreed.

"I saw something on the news about people being kidnapped," Iola said. "I just never thought—" She let out a choked sob, then wailed, "What are we going to do?"

Reaching out, I felt around for her hand and took it in mine as I scooted closer to hug her. "Don't worry, okay? We'll all get through this. We just have to pick the right moment to get us out of this situation."

"When will that be?" Jenny asked.

"I'll only know when the time comes. We'll stay on guard, be good, and figure things out as we go. But most of all we need to do as they say until we can best them."

"How do you sound... unfazed by this?" Cal questioned.

"I—" When our container moved, and a gasp escaped me while the other women screamed.

"What the fuck!" Cal yelled.

"Stay still. If I were to guess, we're in a shipping container and we're being placed on a boat. Prepare for the landing, people," I warned. The metal walls groaned as we tilted, swaying gently from side to side. A hollow clang echoed through the space, followed by a jarring thud that rattled my bones and made me grit my teeth. Dust drifted from somewhere, tickling my nose. "Everyone okay?" I asked.

Jenny answered first, then Cal, and I gently squeezed Iola to me.

"I'm scared," she admitted.

Rubbing up and down her arm, I said, "I know. But we'll get through this."

"How can you be so sure?" Cal demanded, but again, before I could answer, the doors swung open.

We blinked at the light, hands up to protect our eyes. I quickly took in the people with me. Cal was a stunning man with the same dark brown hair as mine. He was the tallest out of us, and I was the shortest. Jenny and Iola were nearly the same height and had blonde hair and blue eyes.

"Up and out. Now," a masked man ordered while pointing his gun at us.

I helped Iola and Jenny up as Cal climbed to his feet. Together, we shuffled outside.

My breath caught.

Surrounding us were more shipping containers and the evening sky.

"In," he ordered, pointing to a bigger container.

Should I ask questions?

"What is this?" Cal suddenly demanded. He got hit in the back of the head and let out a pained sound.

"Quiet."

Another masked man opened the doors to the bigger container and waited for us to enter. I jolted when the doors slammed behind us and spun to see we were trapped once more.

"Rommy," Cal called.

Turning, I gaped at the number of people huddled at the other end. We could only see them because of the dim torch hanging from the ceiling.

There were a few scattered blankets, but that was about it.

Moving forward, I asked, "Are you all from Australia?"

Some called out New South Wales, others Tasmania, and

Queensland, Brisbane, Western Australia... all over the country.

We must have been the last to be picked up.

My stomach tightened at all the fearful gazes.

"Is there a plan?" I asked. "What happens if we need food or the toilet?"

A woman told us, "They take us to the bathroom, but we're only allowed to use the toilet and we're heavily guarded."

"Not everyone goes at the same time," another woman said. "They take us in smaller groups."

A guy shifted on his feet as he said, "Minimal food and water so far. Enough to keep us in the shape we're in."

"I heard them talking about our buyers," another new woman explained as she rubbed her hands nervously together.

The guy next to her nodded. "We were taken to be sold off to the highest bidder unless we already have someone who's willing to pay a large amount up front."

What the fuck?

Buyers?

People still did that?

How did they get away with shit like this?

Goddamn it.

No. I had to stay calm. I had to think.

"Okay. Like I said, we'll just have to wait for the right time to get us out of this situation. No one will be sold if I have anything to do with it," I said.

"Are you a cop?" someone called.

Shaking my head, I shrugged. "Just a person who's had training."

Cal made a grunted noise. "In the other container, you were just as confident we'll get out of this. How can you be so sure? Even if you can fight, there are more of them than there are of us. I know self-defence and can throw a punch, but I doubt everyone does."

So many replied that they didn't know how to fight. But there were a few hopefuls that could help. Jenny was also on that list because she was an ex-police officer.

"What do you know?" Cal asked when everyone had settled down.

"I've been trained in all martial arts. Taught how to use many types of guns and worked with knives."

"Who are you?" another person called.

"I'm Romania, but everyone can call me Rommy. I promise I will do everything in my power to get us out of this."

"No offense, but you're like a..."

Someone else finished: "You're tiny. Who'd be scared of you?"

Smiling, I pressed my hands together under my chin. "I'll make them scared in the end."

"Who taught you all this?" Iola asked.

"My dad and his brothers. They're a part of the Hawks Motorcycle Club."

There were many gasps, and it made me proud that people knew about my family.

"Will they be looking for you?" Cal questioned.

I pushed my shoulders back and said with confidence, "My family will do anything to get me back, and they won't stop until I'm safe. Which means all of you will be safe too. For now, we need to do as they say. We need to stay protected and calm and strong until we can get some help or until we can get off this ship. We'll do recon every time we're let out. I want to know how many guards there are. I know they wear masks, but try and make a note of some type of different feature on them." I took a breath and warned, "In the time we're together, you may think I'm weird or something. I do tend to ramble on about whatever comes to mind, but I promise, you can put your faith in me and my family."

Jenny shifted on her feet. "I trust you, Rommy. She already had a plan when she woke up."

Cal grunted. "Yeah, I believe you." He turned to the others. "She damn near broke my fingers when she woke up in the dark."

Iola took my hand before she softly said, "I trust you."

Smiling, I squeezed her hand. "Thank you." I curled an arm around her shoulders and addressed everyone again. "In one way or another, we will get through this."

There was a huff and then a guy said, "I want to trust you, but you could be making all this up just to be in charge." He stepped forward. "She's probably saying this so we give her extra rations or to have more blankets." He turned to me again. "We were the first here. We get to pick who gets what and what we do."

There was a nod from a couple of them.

A woman stood by this guy. "Trevor is right. Just because she says the right things doesn't mean we should fold to whatever she says." She thumbed at herself and then pointed to the guy. "We're the ones in charge. We're the ones who will get us out of here."

Calmly, I asked, "Can you fight?"

She sneered. "It doesn't have to come down to fighting. There'll be a chance we can escape and then—"

"Be shot down while we all run. I don't want just some of you safe. I want all of you protected." I looked to the other two. "Will you both throw yourselves in front of danger for the other people in here?"

Trevor snorted. "Like you would."

Sighing, I shook my head. "We're in a bad situation, and I really don't want there to be fighting between us. With the training I've had, I'm more than comfortable to be the first and only one to run into danger if it means all of us get to safety."

"She probably doesn't even know how to fight," the woman said.

"What's your name?" I asked.

"Pamela."

"Pamela, do *you* know how to fight?"

"I do boxing."

"Then come at me and throw a punch. Actually, both of you try to hit me." I gently moved Iola out of the way and closer to Cal and Jenny.

Couldn't they see I really didn't want to be in charge but would if it meant I could save everyone?

"Rommy," Cal shouted as he gripped Iola's arm to drag her back.

I'd already felt the shift in the air and ducked while sweeping my leg out. Pamela dropped to the steel floor.

Foolish move, girl.

I popped back up just as Trevor went to jab me in the gut.

Oof, that'll bruise.

But I pushed the pain back and moved.

Grabbing his fist with my left, I uppercut him with my right, and he stumbled back.

"I can do this for hours," I told them, hoping they'd quit wasting energy. "But can we please just get through this together? I won't lord over anyone or anything. I just want to help and get out of here with all of us in one piece."

Trevor helped Pamela up, both glowering at me. They could hate me all they wanted. They'd eventually see it'd be me or my family and friends who'd get us out of this mess. I could already tell they wouldn't be the type of people to say thank you either. Hell, they were also the type to be mean to waitstaff. I hated when people did that.

"Fine," Trevor clipped, and Pamela just nodded.

God, I hoped I didn't just screw up by taking charge, but I really did honestly believe that I could get us out of this somehow. I'd fight as hard as my family would be back home.

CHAPTER FOUR

"I miss salt and vinegar chips," Jenny said.

"Burger Rings," another shouted.

There was a moan close by. "Choc-chip cookies."

"Barbeque Shapes," a new voice added.

I groaned, my mouth watering. What I wouldn't give for any of those right now. "Yes. They're the best, but I love chicken ones too."

Cal, who was on my other side, gently slapped his hand against my leg. "The cheese one." We all groaned.

"I miss showers," Iola said. She was tucked between Jenny and me to keep her warm. We were supposed to be sleeping. It was our turn, but my stomach was eating itself, and we couldn't stop daydreaming about the things we wished we had.

I hummed. "A nice warm shower with soap and shampoo and conditioner."

"And clothes that don't stink of sweat and other things," Cal added.

Laughing, I nodded. "At least we're used to the smells now."

We'd been on the ship for twenty days and were all going a little stir-crazy.

"I'd give my soul to have a nice, juicy, fat steak," someone else said.

I licked my dry lips. "Oh God, or a hamburger with cheese and tomatoes and lettuce."

"And onions," someone called.

"Don't forget the sauce," Cal said.

There were a few laughs around the container.

"You lot need to sleep. If you're not going to, we will," Pamela called from up near the door where she and others were on guard duty. All of us couldn't sleep at the same time, so it was their turn to listen near the entrance in case something happened and then they could wake the rest of us.

Sighing, I sat up. "I'm not ready to sleep anyway."

"Rommy, you need to," Jenny said.

Standing, I moved out of the way. "I'll be okay. Cal, you move over to Iola." She was still shivering a bit so she needed all the body heat she could get. "Does anyone on watch want to nap?"

"Lessa, you go get rest," Pamela ordered.

"Glad to," Lessa said, and we swapped ends.

I sat on the steel floor near the doors. There were nine others, and we'd be the next to go out to the bathroom when the masked men came to get us. Though, with the amount of water we drank, which was hardly any, we didn't need to go often. But still, it was good to stretch our legs outside with some fresh air.

I often thought about my family. About how they were dealing, what were they doing, and what did they have for dinner or lunch or breakfast.

God, I'd sell a body part for an iced chocolate.

So far, the masked men had been manageable to deal with. They still needed to be punished for taking us, for putting us through this vile ordeal that made me angry and sick and confused and upset and feel too much all at the same time where I had to take big gulps of air to control the anger burning under my skin, pushing me to lash out.

But I couldn't.

It wasn't the time.

Will it ever be the time?

Yes, it would. I had to have faith.

Something would happen, and that was when I'd act.

So even though the masked men never touched us—they just leered or threatened or shoved us if we moved too slow—they'd still pay for being involved.

Great, now I'd worked myself up. I needed to burn off some energy to stop all the thoughts rushing through my mind. I rolled, slapping my hands to the steel floor and straightening myself out into a plank.

"One," I muttered to myself, counting each push-up to settle my mind.

Pamela scoffed. "Don't you ever stop?"

No, I didn't.

I couldn't.

If I stopped, I'd be lost to all my thoughts, and my mind wouldn't shut up. I'd overthink something too much, which could lead to a mistake.

Working out helped keep me fit and calmed my mind.

I didn't exercise for whoever my buyer was.

The guards had been talking the other day just outside the doors when we'd learned that a lot of us did have "owners," in America. I was one of them, and the owners had somehow seen a photo or a newspaper article or a website and had wanted to own us for whatever perverted reason they had.

We'd never see them, though.

I'd make sure of it somehow.

Still, I hoped that the organisers and whoever these buyers were got taught a lesson. One that involved a lot of pain.

I could be vicious when I wanted to be. When certain times called for it. Like this situation.

But most of the time I was as sweet as pie. I loved life and people and food.

God, I wanted food.

Mashed potatoes.

Carbonara.

Chicken schnitzel.

Pizza.

Vegemite on toast with cheese and melty butter.

But for now, I just had to keep staying strong.

I stilled for a moment when I heard footsteps approaching. I stood as the door rattled and then swung open.

"Bathroom" was snapped.

I helped the others around me to stand, and we filed out in one line.

Drawing in a deep breath, I followed Pamela at the front as we walked silently through the piles of shipping containers to the door that led us inside the ship.

So far on this trip, I had counted twenty masked men lingering around with guns. Watching us like they were waiting for us to act up. But I'd made all the others promise no one would step out and risk harm to themselves or anyone else.

Even Pamela and Trevor had agreed to that.

We took turns using the toilet, but while waiting, I saw at least another ten guards I hadn't noticed before, each with something different to the others we'd already made mental notes about. I was sure there were a lot more manning the ship too. So, for a rough guess, I'd put the count at fifty.

Fifty men.

If I had their weapons and took some hostages, I could possibly pull off a takeover.

And hopefully survive it all at the same time.

My belly twisted in fear, but I wouldn't let it stop me from doing what I had to.

There would be help on the other end. My family would have figured out that we were headed for the US, and they'd either be there waiting for me or have someone they knew and trusted there to help all of us to get free.

I believed it.

Which was why I'd be fighting on my end, too, no matter how nervous or scared I'd be.

CHAPTER FIVE

It was time. I bounced on my feet and stretched my arms in front of me while waiting with Cal and Jenny by the doors for the right moment.

We'd been in this shipping container for forty-seven long days. But that would end today.

A few of us had heard the masked guards talking about the ship docking to pick up the last of the "merchandise" before moving on to our final destination.

Final destination. I liked those movies even though they scared me.

But back to the matter at hand. I knew with every bone in my body that if we reached the place where our "owners" were, we'd be shit out of luck trying to save ourselves.

This was our only chance, and I was pumped for it.

I was tired of sitting back and waiting and pretending to be compliant.

I wanted to bring the hurt.

I wanted to war with all these men who thought they were allowed to take us, push us, starve us, and sell us.

They'd pay. I'd make sure of it, and then I could get home for that family dinner at my brother's so he could announce Maya's pregnancy. He'd better not have told anyone without me there. I wanted to see Mum's face. I knew she'd be over-the-moon happy with a grandbaby.

That was if Maya was pregnant.

I was at least 80 percent sure she was.

"Again, you two don't have to help," I told Cal and Jenny.

Cal snorted. "You're not doing this on your own."

"Cal's right. The others don't have any skills in fighting like us. I know we're not anywhere near as good as you, but we can help," Jenny said.

"Thanks, guys."

Iola was with the other captives, huddled closer to the back of the shipping container with the torch off so they wouldn't be seen when the doors opened.

Movement outside had settled, and the ship was no longer swaying in the ocean, so we were already docked. It was just a waiting game now.

I hated waiting.

It was boring.

I wanted to move. To make waves so we could get out of here and be around the ones we loved. My family would be going crazy.

Hell, it really wouldn't surprise me if they were out there waiting for us or had gotten someone to come help us escape.

Still, I wouldn't sit around and wait to be saved. I'd do

everything I could to make sure all of us were okay in the end.

I heard voices outside the doors.

"Shhh," I called.

They opened with a creak and clang. Five masked guards with two captives appeared.

Two men.

They were shoved inside, and a guard I didn't recognise said something before he walked off. The new men huddled close to the side of the container, and another masked man was about to close the doors.

I couldn't lose this chance. Starting forward, I called, "Hey, hi, hello. Can I use the toilet, pretty please? I really need to go, and I don't want to pee in here." As I approached with Cal and Jenny, one of the kidnapped men pressed the younger one back against the wall to stand in front of him. Protecting him. I smiled in reassurance.

"Stop. No break," a guard barked, pointing his gun my way. "Stay back," he warned.

Jenny and Cal stepped out of the shadows and stopped behind me.

Using my thumb, I pointed over my shoulder to my friends and walked closer. "I know it's early for a toilet break, but we really gotta go. We'll be good."

Before he could respond, I rushed him.

In one fluid move, I shot my arm out to grab his wrist. With a twist of my body, I spun him around, using his momentum against him. I slammed my foot into his back and sent him stumbling straight into Cal and Jenny, who were ready for him. I trusted that they could take care of him while I moved on.

Like the Flash—at least I liked to think so—I charged the remaining two guards.

"Stop! I'll shoot," one of them shouted, and I grinned at the panic edging his voice.

Only I didn't even pause as I sprang at him, climbing his body like a jungle gym—one foot on his thigh, the other on his chest. Then I snapped my leg around his neck, and with a powerful arch of my back, I flipped him off his feet and drove him into the metal floor. He hit the ground hard, choking and flailing as I cinched my leg tighter around his throat like a vice.

The last masked guard took a step forward with his gun trembling in his hands.

I almost laughed at his fear of little old me, but I kept it locked inside. "I don't want to shoot you," I told him calmly. "Drop your weapon."

"Get off him! Stand down!" he yelled back.

Shit. His finger tightened on the trigger.

The man under me thrashed wildly—clawing, slapping at my thigh, his face reddening.

His actions hurt, but I ignored them. I had to get this scene under control.

Refusing to react, I repeated my words more harshly, "I said drop it."

If only he'd listen.

Sighing, I shook my head and then pressed my hand against my leg to tighten the chokehold I already had on the guy under me with my leg.

I glanced down when he bucked before passing out.

My gaze snagged on the blade at his hip. Reaching down, I yanked it free, and with a flick of my wrist, I threw the knife. It spun through the air before sinking into the last guard's hand.

He screamed as he dropped his gun and clutched his bleeding palm to his chest.

I did warn him.

"Stay still, please," I said, rising to my feet, pointing the unconscious guard's gun at the whimpering man. "Cal, take his weapon and watch him."

My friend nodded and moved quickly to help.

BANG. BANG. BANG.

Repeated shots were fired, and screams started from deeper within the container.

In a panic, I ordered, "We need to leave. Cal, Jenny, round everyone up."

"Wait," one of the new guys called. He walked towards me, holding the other younger guy's hand. "That will be my family. My man, he was here hiding with the Diamond MC and—"

Hope bloomed, and I blurted, "Get the fuck outta here. The Diamond MC? I've heard of them. I overheard my dad talking about our club doing a favour for yours."

The man gaped. "Romania?"

Smiling, I told him, "Rommy for short. Oh wow, oh wow, is that why you guys are here? Did Dad call in a favour to help me? Aww, that's the sweetest thing."

See, I knew my family would help. They were the best.

"Oui, chéri. Our family was already here to help everyone when Sawyer and I, Henri"—he touched his chest —"were taken."

"I like your accent. French, right? I've always wanted to

learn it." Groaning inwardly, I smacked my palm to my forehead. I could be a fool sometimes. I quickly said, "But now's not the time to talk about it. Will your guys be easy to notice?"

"Oui, they won't wear masks and will have the biker vests on. Except my man, Blaze, he's a really big man and probably the one going crazy on the kidnappers."

He sounded like my kind of guy. I wanted to get out there to see for myself. "Cool, cool. I'm gonna go see how things are travelling. See if they need help." I checked the gun for bullets. "How about you all stay here and watch these idiots?" Glaring down, I kicked out at the one who'd passed out to check he wasn't faking. "He's still out. Good. I'll bring your guy back?"

He paused, looking at the guard and then at me. "Oh, oui. Thank you."

"You got it." I faced Cal and Jenny, who were now smiling as they stood armed over the ship crew. I grinned. "We're getting out of here. Yay!" I cheered before I took off running.

I could have cried knowing we weren't alone. We had help, and from the sound of it, there were a lot assisting in our rescue.

Rounding a corner, I saw chaos. So much fighting, but it was slowing down. There weren't many masked guards left to deal with.

Pity, but I was grateful since I'd been worried I couldn't have handled everyone on my own.

A big guy in a club vest caught my attention when he yelled in the face of his opponent as he wrapped his hands around the guy's neck.

However, he also left himself unprotected and was about to get a knife to the back.

Launching myself forward, I hit the guard in the side of the head with the back of my gun and watched him fall to the floor unconscious. Bending, I checked his pulse, which still ticked away, before bouncing up to my feet and noticing how quiet it'd gone around me.

Waving, I announced, "Hey, hi, hello, hot biker guys. I'm Romania. But call me Rommy. You might be here to save me? I have the others who were kidnapped in the back." I shot finger guns at the massive, good-looking guy I just saved. "Dude, you need to remember to watch your back." Then I pointed at the other guy, who was bigger than my dude and looked ready to murder some more people, and said, "You've got to be Henri's beau. Come on. I can tell you need to see him." I tipped my head back. "This way. Wait, does my dad know I'm okay?"

Another biker brother, who was holding an iPad, stepped forward. "I've just messaged them. They know we've got the ship under control."

Tension drained from my body. "Thanks heaps." I imagined they'd already be heading to the airport to get here to me, so I didn't even need to ask. Instead, I waved Blaze over. "Come on. You're barely hanging on. Your Henri is this way."

The big broody brute followed me silently with two others. The one I'd saved and another brother, who looked worried about something or someone.

Blaze was almost vibrating with tension. "Don't worry, big man," I told him as we walked. "He's just down here. Once you see he's fine, you can settle down."

He didn't respond, which was fine and understandable. He wanted his eyes on his man.

I glanced to the other two and couldn't help but say to the one I'd saved, "Hot damn, you're just as big as Blaze, aren't you?" When he said nothing, I laughed as I skipped through the gap first. When Blaze and his brothers walked through, I gestured to the hostages. "See, all safe."

No one said anything. They all stood there staring. I watched back and forth between Henri, Blaze, and the biker brothers. The one with darker hair was looking at Sawyer, Henri's friend, with concern. Were they an item?

Yet, they were still standing around like they had all the time in the world.

They didn't.

I wanted to get everyone somewhere we could shower, eat, drink, and sleep knowing we were safe.

"So," I drew out. "Is this standoff normal?"

The smoking-hot guy I saved snorted. "Give them a moment." I glanced down at his nametag on his club cut. Quake.

"Mon amour?" Henri said.

Blaze's jaw clenched again, but he unlocked it to order, "Here. Now."

Henri ran at him and jumped into his arms. My heart warmed at the scene.

I moved closer to Quake and nudged his side with my elbow. "Aww, they're so cute together. Don't you think?"

He coughed and hesitantly said, "Ah, yeah."

Laughing, I told him, "You're cute too."

The big guy blushed before he turned around and

started walking back the way we came when he called, "I'm goin' to check on the brothers."

I'd worm my way into his heart, and bed, if I was lucky enough.

But for now, I really wanted to get things moving.

Clapping, I asked, "Right, who wants to get out of here? I really gotta call my dad soon before he shits kittens. The tech guy said they messaged him I was found and safe, but he'll want to hear my voice." I waved my hand towards the exit. "Let's go, people. Time's wasting. We need food and water and definitely showers. Huh, maybe that's why that guy ran off quickly." I lifted my arm and sniffed under my armpit, then screwed up my nose at the stink. "Yeah, that's rank." I moved up behind Blaze. "Hey, big man. Just gonna put my hands on your waist and help you step to the side so people can get past. You just keep breathing in your man and calming down." Before I did, I looked to Henri, who nodded, so I placed my hands on him so people could walk by.

Finally, we were free.

Stepping off the ship for the first time in over a month was the best feeling. I smiled widely at everyone around me.

"Rommy," Cal called. He stood with Jenny, Iola, and another man. I went over and hugged them. Except the stranger, though I'd have if I'd known him or if he wanted a hug.

Pulling back, I gripped Iola and Jenny's hand. "We're free."

They grinned, and Cal nodded with a bright grin. "We are."

"Thanks to you," Iola said.

"Rommy, this is Officer Jones." Jenny dropped my hand to gesture to the cop. "He's here to help all of us get home again and to stay protected until the ones behind this are taken care of."

Nodding, I smiled up at the cop. "Thank you."

"These three hold you in high regard, Romania. Thanks for helping keep everyone safe."

I shrugged. "I only did what any person would."

"Rommy." A man with a wicked beard and 'stache walked up. The name on his club vest read *Country*. He was the president to the Diamond MC. "You'll come with us. Your family will arrive at our compound tomorrow evening."

"You got it." I winked. Facing Cal, Iola, and Jenny again, I gave them a sad smile. "I guess this is goodbye."

"Not forever," Cal said quickly. "You're stuck with us for life."

Tears sprang to life, and my gaze blurred. "I wouldn't want it any other way. Does anyone have a pen and paper?" I called. The officer produced one, and I wrote down my number, passing it to my friends. "Call me. Anytime. Love you, guys." I hugged them tightly before stepping back. With a big wave where I stretched my arm all the way up, I called. "Bye, everyone. Take care."

There were a lot of farewells before I turned and made my way to the car with Country. I felt dead on my feet, but the excitement of seeing the Diamond MC compound and meeting more amazing people gave me enough energy to keep my eyes open. Plus, I knew I'd be getting food soon, and I really couldn't wait for that. Just the thought had my mouth pooling with saliva.

CHAPTER SIX

Sleep evaporated, and I stretched on the bed before moaning from how good it felt. Opening my eyes, I took in the room and remembered where I was. With a smile, I did a wiggle at the thought of not waking in that damn stinky shipping container.

Sure, I missed my friends, but I wouldn't want to go back in time to be with them in there again. And since Cal, Jenny, Iola, and I had all been from Melbourne, we could easily catch up when we got back to town.

I was surprised I didn't have nightmares or some type of fear over the whole ordeal. Maybe if I were anyone else but myself, I would have. Instead, the positives outweighed anything else I'd been put through. Yes, we went without a lot on the ship, but I knew help would come. I knew we would get out of it because I believed in my family.

And maybe that was what helped keep the fear and nightmares at bay.

Then again, my mind was wired different too.

Sitting, I pushed the blankets away and turned before dropping my feet to the wood floor. It was a little chilly this morning... wait, it was morning, right? I glanced to the digital clock on the bedside table. Nine in the morning. Perfect time to grab some much-needed food. Mum always said I woke hungry like a bear.

Mum. On the boat, I'd missed her and Dad and everyone all the time. They must have been going nuts to find me. I couldn't wait to see them later tonight. The phone call on the drive to the compound wasn't enough. I needed to have them in front of me. At least now they didn't have to worry. Dad trusted the Diamond MC, so I would too.

Though, they'd already made it easy to trust them for coming to the rescue and then taking good care of me last night.

Dusty, Country's old lady, had fed me when we got to the compound before showing me to a spare room where I crashed big time since the adrenaline had worn off.

Now it was a new day.

A better day because I was free and happy and surrounded by people who were awesome. I couldn't wait to get to know them. I'd met a few when I'd walked in last night, but I didn't really take in any faces or names.

I headed to the attached bathroom and took another shower. I'd had one before I climbed into the bed last night, which had felt like heaven. Even now I grinned as I dropped my head back and let the droplets run over my face.

But then coughed and spluttered when some of the water slipped up my nose to run down my throat.

Laughing at myself, I finished washing and then dried off before wrapping the same towel around my hair while I looked through the clothing options. Dusty had given me some items that belonged to a woman named Eve. However, I didn't feel comfortable wearing someone else's undies, so I went commando with the wide-legged, black tracksuit pants and a black, tight, long-sleeved, cotton top. With them, I put on nice thick socks.

The fresh clothing felt snuggly and warm. On the boat, we'd had many nights huddled together to try and stay warm from each other's body heat, so it was good to have that toasty feeling again. The day I'd been taken I'd only been wearing jeans and a tee, which hadn't been comfortable to stay in for a month.

Removing the towel from my hair, I went back in the bathroom to hang it and brushed my long locks. Dusty had also been a gem to find me a new hairbrush, toothbrush, and toothpaste. She'd asked me if I wanted make-up, but when she saw my screwed-up nose at that offer, she smiled and told me I was naturally pretty without it anyway, which was sweet.

Not that I saw the appeal with my looks. I always thought my eyes and lips were too big. But if people found me nice to look at, I wasn't going to question them about it.

Once ready, I made my way out of the room and down the stairs. I walked straight into the common room area, which was a lot busier than it had been last night.

"Hey, hi, hello, everyone." I waved when I came to a stop at the bottom of the staircase. The room went quiet, so I, of course, felt the need to fill that silence. "For those who I didn't meet— Actually, I was in a bit of a daze last night so I might not remember who I met, which is why I'll just let you all know, I'm Romania, but you can call me

Rommy. My dad runs the Caroline Springs chapter of the Hawks Motorcycle Club in Melbourne, Australia." When no one said anything, I did. "I'm a mechanic. I like working on cars, but I prefer bikes. I like reading romance books that steam up the pages, and I... am rambling because I'm nervous, sort of, or just feeling like I'm making this more awkward than it should have been. Anyway, thank you for coming to the rescue at the shipping container." With that, I bowed. I didn't know why, but I just did it, and when I popped back up, I smiled and shot finger guns.

Kill me now.

"Can someone show me where the food is, please?" I begged.

Dusty stepped forward with a smile. "Morning, Rommy."

I quickly made my way over to her for a hug.

"Hey. Sorry about all that. I can word vomit like a pro sometimes, but I also like talking, and I tend to say whatever's on my mind, so I'm sorry if I say anything wrong."

Her smile was warm. "Don't worry about it, okay? You just be yourself here."

"Thanks. I really like all your accents too. They sound so cool."

"I think yours sounds better," she said just as a woman stepped up. Even with the glare, she was beautiful with her blonde hair just past her shoulders and baby blues. Dusty smiled at her. "Rommy, this is Eve—"

"Oh, hey," I said as I pulled her into a hug, which she didn't return and stayed stiff for. When I pulled back, she just blinked at me as I added, "Thanks for the clothes, and it's so nice to meet you. Are you an old lady to one of the brothers?"

Eve blinked again. "You're like an Energizer Bunny."

Smiling, I nodded and shrugged. "I have been told that. If I get to be too much, just let me know and I can shut up or I'll take a walk away from you. I don't want to annoy you or anyone for that matter."

"It's fine. And no, I'm not an old lady. Tech's my brother."

"Oh, cool." I nodded. "I have a brother too. His name's Texas. Look at that. Both our brother's names start with T."

"Ah, yeah." She looked at Dusty. "I'm heading out."

Dusty nodded. "I might not be here later. Have fun at work."

"Yeah, I'll try," she replied.

"See you later," I said before she nodded and walked away. I wasn't sure she liked me too much or appreciated my hug. "I shouldn't have hugged her, right? I can't help myself. I'm a hugger. I like people, but I have to remember not everyone likes to be hugged."

"Don't worry about it. Eve's... she's never really been one to want affection or touch from people, no matter who they are."

That made my heart clench. I wanted to shower Eve with so much affection, but I had to be respectful, so I wouldn't crowd her. Something in Eve's life made her not want touch or affection, and I was sure that whatever it was, wasn't good.

"Come on. Let's get some food into you. Do you want a coffee?" Dusty asked as she placed her hand to my back to steer me towards double swinging doors.

"Ha. If I have a coffee, I'll be bouncing off the walls and talking more than I am now. No one needs that."

"There's nothing wrong with wanting to say things, Rommy."

Dusty was the sweetest. No wonder Country snapped her up.

"Thanks, Dusty." When we walked through the doors, I stopped and gaped at all the goodies on the kitchen counter. Silver trays of scrambled eggs, bacon, some type of bread, sausages, muffins, and then there was boxes and boxes of cereal.

Saliva pooled in my mouth.

"Rommy?" Dusty asked. I wasn't sure if her calling my name was the first time or not.

"Food," I commented.

I loved me some food.

Dusty laughed. "Grab a plate and help yourself. There's a drink area on the table over there."

Nodding, I practically floated over and took a plate to pile the food high on.

I'd just picked up a large blueberry muffin when the back door opened and my wet dream walked in.

Quake stepped through and stopped when he saw me.

"Hi," I said around my mouthful, which I quickly finished chewing and swallowing. "The food looks amazing. Have you had breakfast? You better get in here before I eat it all." I took another big bite as I watched him glance from my mouth to my plate, to the food, and then back to my plate. I shrugged. "Who doesn't love food, right? I'd eat anything. What about you?"

"Yeah," he said slowly.

"Quake, have you met Rommy?"

"We didn't *officially* meet, but I saw and admired him yesterday." I stuffed the muffin in my mouth and held out my hand while Dusty giggled.

Quake closed the back door and moved my way to take my hand. "Rommy, right?"

I nodded. When he released my hold, I bit off some more blueberry goodness, and around it, I asked, "Who makes all this stuff?"

Dusty turned from the table where the drinks sat. "I love baking. I do most, but I also have the help of the club girls."

I could feel Quake studying me. Was he waiting on a reaction from me about the club girls?

"Cool. Mum gets the girls in the compound to help out too. They can't just laze about while waiting for the guys, am I right?"

"Exactly," Dusty said.

I glanced and smiled at Quake, who was staring at me.

The doors behind us opened, and more bikers filed in. One was Tech. "You're Eve's brother."

He smirked. "Twin brother."

"No shit."

He chuckled. "No shit."

I turned to the other guy. "Hey, I saw you on the boat yesterday too. I'm Rommy." This guy had been unhinged on the boat going from one to another and taking them down without a care in the world. I didn't miss the blood that had coated him.

The buzzcut guy nodded. "Torch."

"Cool. Like that name." I nodded just as something slipped by Torch's legs. I cried, "Puppy." I quickly placed my plate to the counter before I went to the floor and opened my arms.

"No!" Tech yelled.

"Harley," Torch barked.

And before the puppy could reach me, I was picked up off the floor with an arm around my waist. I glanced over my shoulder and patted the big guy's arm. "I'm good, Quake. He's just a puppy."

I could feel how fast he was breathing. "That dog only likes two people. Torch and his old lady, Wrenley. He sometimes tolerates Tech and Death, since they on occasion look after him. But the beast doesn't like anyone else."

I snorted and rolled my eyes as I tapped his arm. "Animals love me." I wiggled against Quake who grunted. "Any other time we can play, but I wanna see the puppy."

Next, I was dropped like a sack of hot potatoes, and Quake moved away with burning cheeks.

Aww, he was too cute. Would he blush if I got naked?

Not that I'd do that. At least not with this many people around and especially if there were brothers who had old ladies. Getting naked in front of taken men would be disrespectful, and I'd never do that.

"What are you thinkin'?" Tech asked.

"That I wouldn't get naked in front of anyone who's in a relationship." I dropped down to my knees again and looked up at Torch. "Can he come closer?"

Torch glanced down to Harley, who was sitting at his side. He tipped his chin my way and then Harley placed his attention on me.

"Come on, cutie. Who's such a good boy? Yes, you are," I cooed, holding out my hands. He drew closer and sniffed at my hands. "You're such a handsome boy, Harley. I bet your mum and dad take good care of such a sweet boy." His tail started wagging. Then he got the bum wiggle going before jumping at me to lick my face. Laughing, I patted him all over. "Yes, I knew you were a nice boy."

Tech sighed. "Fuckin' women and animals. You'd probably try and pet a bear, too, right?"

Grinning, I shrugged as I rubbed my hands over Harley, who now sat in front of me. "Probably."

"When the guys found Harley, he wasn't in a good place. He went to attack Death, but Torch got him to the ground first, and since then they've had this bond," Dusty explained.

I nodded. "Torch is the alpha, isn't he, Harley?" He licked up my nose, making me giggle. I kissed him right back on the snout before I stood. "I've got to finish my brekkie. I'll play later," I told Harley with one final pat.

"Brekkie?" Quake asked.

"Yeah, short for breakfast. Us Aussies like to shorten any word we can." I walked over to the sink to wash my hands with soap. Usually, I wouldn't give two hoots if I had dog all over my hands, I'd still eat with them, but I didn't want to give off a bad image. Not yet. They were still getting to know me. After I dried them, I went to pick up my plate again to finish off the blueberry muffin.

A moan slipped out. I waited until I finished chewing for once before I said, "I forgot how good food tasted. Well, I'm gonna go sit down. My mum always said it's better to sit and eat than stand. Don't ask me why, though. She never told me when I asked." I glanced to Dusty. "Are you coming back out?"

With a smile, she nodded.

"Later, guys," I called before leaving.

When I sat at a table, Dusty introduced me to Saint, Gun, Lucas, Wreck, Death, and Raya.

"Damn, the fairy Godmother blessed all these bikers with the good-looking stick too."

Lucas waved his hand. "I'm not a biker." Wreck's palm slid to the back of Lucas's neck, under all his blond curls.

"Ah, you just belong to a biker."

Lucas smiled and nodded.

"I'm also his blood brother," Saint said. "Now, after you finish eatin', I'd like to pick your brain about your mechanical skills."

I squinted at him with my fork full of scrambled eggs halfway to my mouth. "You don't have anyone in the club working on your babies?"

"We did, but he left the club a while ago. We take them to a place close by."

"That sucks. We have a garage connected to the compound, and a lot of the brothers work there."

Wreck grunted. "We know how to fix some things, but not every detail."

I pointed my fork his way. "Gotcha. Look, I'm happy to answer any questions about anything. I'm not really shy—"

"You're kiddin'," Saint teased.

He and Gun chuckled when I gave him the middle finger with a smile. "As you can probably tell, I'm not shy, but I can put my foot in my mouth a lot of the time. So, tell me if I'm overstepping in any way."

"I heard you warn Dusty about yourself before," Gun said. "Don't worry about what anyone thinks of you,

Rommy. If they don't like you, that's a them problem, not you."

My heart swelled, as I grinned big. "Thanks heaps. That means a lot. Like *a lot*."

Dusty rested her hand on my arm. "Honestly, Rommy, just make yourself at home here, and don't worry about anyone, okay?"

I gave her a watery smile. "I'll try."

She returned my smile with her own and nodded. "Good."

She said to make myself at home here, but even when I walked through the door last night, the place had the same feeling the compound did at home. So, I could already tell I was going to love my stay. Now, if only I could talk my parents into taking a holiday so we could stick around for a while to get to know everyone.

CHAPTER SEVEN

The day had been full and fun. I got to see Henri and Sawyer, who had both been kidnapped. They were with Henri's man, Blaze, and little Arlo. They made such a sweet family. It had made my heart ache from wanting to see my own.

However, until they arrived, I'd kept myself busy getting to know Saint and Gun more while they took me on a tour of the compound outside where their stunning rides sat. Saint was true to his word and had picked my brain about his bike. The more I told him what I could do to her, the more he got giddy over the ideas while Gun watched him with amusement.

I loved that this club was like my family's and didn't discriminate on the brothers loving who they wanted.

But being surrounded by awesome people all day really did make me miss my people from home.

Saint snorted when I glanced at the clock on the wall

again. I shoved him. "I should have gone with Country to pick them up."

"Nah, it's probably best the tearful reunion is here than at the airport."

Nodding, I picked up the controller to the gaming system again. Earlier, when Saint had asked if I gamed and he saw my excited look, he'd taken me to this bedroom, and since then, we'd been playing.

"You've got a good set-up here," I told him as I pressed the button to start another race.

Saint grabbed the other gamepad. "It ain't mine."

I stopped, saw my character crash, and looked to Saint. "Whose room are we in? Will they mind us being in here? If they're anything like my brother, I know he doesn't like his things being touched and would kick anyone's arse if he caught us. Will my arse be kicked? If they come for me, Saint, I'm totally throwing you under the bus and claiming innocence since I am actually innocent. You should have told me this room wasn't yours. Why was the door wide open when we got here? Anyone could just stroll in like we did."

Saint roared with laughter, his whole body shaking. He patted my thigh when he started to calm down. "Relax, Rommy."

"Relax? Sure, okay. I'll totally relax because you said so."

He grinned wide. "This is Quake's room, and he leaves his door open so the brothers who want a little downtime can come in here to play with his set-up."

Quake's? That made me want to study every detail in the room, but first I had to make sure I'd be welcomed in my wet dream's space. "Saint. Did you by any chance notice that I'm not a brother? I don't have a peen between my legs, so are you completely sure I'm welcome in that luscious man's area?"

Saint laughed again. "Luscious? Quake?"

I gave him wide eyes. "Ah, yes."

He snorted. "Sure, Rommy." He made it sound like I needed to get my head checked. The time to do that was long past. "But to answer your question, Quake won't care you're in here playing. He and Dusty used to game a lot before she and Country became joined at the hip."

"Dusty games? I'll have to ask her to play when she's got some free time." She had a baby boy bundle of joy to take care of when she wasn't cooking or running the club house with Country.

"Yeah. She's pretty good at it too."

"Cool, cool." Nodding, I grabbed the controller once more and sat back on the couch. "All right, you ready to lose again?"

"I won the last game."

"Only because you cheated." I glanced at the clock again.

He scoffed. "I don't cheat. I'm just that good."

A knock sounded, and we looked to the doorway where Quake leaned.

I dropped the gamepad on the couch and stood. Pointing down at Saint, I yelled, "He dragged me in here to play the games."

Saint snorted before scrubbing a hand over his face.

Quake grinned for the first time. Immediately, my heart stumbled over a beat as my belly fluttered. He was already stunning, but when he smiled, it made me want to throw a bag over his head so no one else saw how special it was.

"You're droolin'," Saint muttered out the corner of his mouth.

Kicking back, I hit him in the shin.

"All good." My attention went to Quake as soon as I heard his low rumble. "Anyone can game. I just stopped by to let you know your family's here."

Pumping the air, I cried, "Yes," then bolted out of the room.

My family, my family, my family.

Tears filled my eyes, but I was smiling too. I wanted to hug Mum and Dad so damn bad.

I was halfway down the hallway when I heard Quake call, "Wrong way."

Turning, I raced by Quake and Saint and made my way to the stairs. When I heard the voices, I took two at a time. Familiar voices that had my heart clenching.

Voices I missed and loved.

At the bottom of the stairs, the crowd parted to reveal Mum and Dad.

I gripped at the material on my chest as I grinned and let the tears fall.

"Kid, get your arse over here," Dad ordered.

With a sob, I ran at them and barrelled into their bodies as we wrapped each other up. I clung to them both, burying my face into their arms.

"Fuck," Dad clipped, voice tight with emotions. His hand cupped the back of my head, and I felt him kiss against my hair. "Christ, Rommy."

"I know," I whispered. "I know."

"Holy goddamn shit," Mum cried, hugging me tighter. "My baby girl. Scared the life outta me."

"I'm sorry."

"Not your fault. Not *anyone's* fault but those fucking monsters who nabbed you." She cupped my cheeks and pulled my head up. "I know you said it, baby girl, but tell me honestly, did they hurt you?"

"No. I promise. They wanted us untouched for our buyers."

Mum's jaw clenched, and she looked over my head. "Tell me we have these fuckers."

"Low," Dad warned. I glanced back to see the Diamond MC president standing with his arms crossed.

"It's fine, Dodge," Country said before he looked at Mum. "We'll make sure their business is shut down one way or another."

Mum nodded and went back to cupping my cheeks. "Did you kick arse?"

Dad groaned and palmed his face while I grinned up at her. "I sure did."

"That's my girl."

"Can I get a hug now?"

My eyes widened. I hadn't noticed anyone else but my parents. They moved to my brother and Maya.

"Guys," I whispered, fresh tears welling.

Texas swallowed thickly as he reached out, snagged my wrist in his hand, and yanked me into him, hugging me tight.

"Fucking hell, Rom. You're never going anywhere on your own. You'll have someone at your back when dealin' with customers too. This shit will never fuckin' happen again."

I nodded against his chest. I didn't care if he organised

someone to glue themselves to me, I knew how worried my family would have been, and I was willing to ease their stress in any way I could until the day I died.

"What are you doing here?" I asked, voice thick with emotions.

He gently smacked the back of my head. "You think I wouldn't come help get my pain-in-the-arse sister from America?" His hands went to my shoulders, and he pushed me back to turn me to where Maya was waiting.

With a watery laugh, I clung to her.

"Thank you for coming," I said.

"Nothing would have stopped us from coming," she said.

With a sniffle, I held her tighter. I really did have the best people in my life.

"I think this calls for a drink," Mum announced.

I moved out of Maya's arms to stand beside her and hold her hand, smiling. My body felt light from seeing my family here with me.

Country chuckled. "Sounds good to me." He turned to the bar and called, "Prospects, take orders." Three guys, who looked a little younger than me, went into action at Country's words.

We were led to a seating area away from the benches where they all sat for dinner. I stood behind the couch and rested my hands on my brother's shoulders where he sat on the sofa with Maya and Mum. Dad was in his own chair and so were Country, Saint, and Wreck.

I saw Mum eyeing Wreck. "Jesus, you're a big one."

Wreck stared at her while I laughed before telling her, "You should see Blaze. He's Henri's guy and ginormous.

Henri, who is French, along with their boy Sawyer, but he's not French, just Henri, got kidnapped and taken to the ship too. You'll get to meet them before we leave hopefully. I really like them. I like everyone here. No one's been a dick, so it's good."

Dad grinned. "Hell, kid, you've been missed."

Lifting my hand, I blew him a kiss.

"Rommy was tellin' us she's a mechanic," Saint said. "She's given me some ideas for my ride, and I'm hopin' she'll be stickin' around long enough to show me."

I'd confessed to Saint that I wished I could stay longer to take in the town and make a family holiday of it. However, I knew Mum and Dad were busy with the club and businesses. Texas also owned a tattoo shop in Ballarat. I couldn't keep them away from their responsibilities.

Not unless it wasn't my idea in the beginning.

Dad shared a look with Mum before he said, "We were hopin' to stick around for a while."

"Really?" I asked loudly while shaking my brother's shoulders.

Dad chuckled. "Not sure about Texas and Maya, though. Low and I are covered for the garage and compound. Texas?"

"My clients understand why I'm not there and that I shut the tattoo shop for at least a week."

Gasping, I shook my brother again. "So, we can all stay for a week, at least?"

"Jesus, Rommy," Texas complained, tapping my hand.

"Oh my God, we can do so much. I've already asked about the places we can go. There're shops, a museum, and nature walks. Mum, I already know you won't be doing those. But there's so much more to do, and we have to try all the food we can while we're here. And then Vegas isn't far away, and we so have to check that out. This is gonna be epic."

"Kid, I think we'll need a little longer than a week to get everythin' in," Dad said.

"What do you mean? What does that mean? Are we staying longer? But Texas—"

"Rom, Maya and I have to head back in a week, but Dodge and Low want to hang longer."

I was already nodding. "Yes. Please. Me too. I'll stay longer. Where are we gonna stay? Is there a hotel close by?"

"We have enough rooms here," Country offered.

Mum and Dad shared a look before Dad said, "Yeah, that'd be cool. It'll give us a chance to get to know each other, and I can help the kid go over some of the rides for whoever is interested."

Mum groaned before she asked Country, "Please tell me your old lady loves to shop?"

Country chuckled. "I'm sure she'd love to take you, and no doubt there'll be more partners willing to go too."

"Do you have them go on their own?" Dad asked.

"There's always someone followin'. That's if West, Lucas, and Gun aren't going. If they are, Adrick and Wreck will tag along."

Wreck grunted.

I cocked my head to the side. "West? I haven't met West yet, right?"

Saint snorted. "Believe me, you'd remember if you had—"

"What the fuck does that mean?" Gun asked as he walked over.

Saint grinned. "Boo, you gettin' jealous?"

"No, dickhead. But explain in long detail what you mean."

I grinned at an amused Mum and Dad as they watched Saint and Gun.

"What I meant, lover, was that you would remember West because he has this Russian dark lord followin' him everywhere."

Gun huffed and sat on the armrest of Saint's chair as Saint wound an arm around Gun's back. "I guess that works."

"I see no one but you and your pretty face," Saint told him, staring up at him with such love it made my heart stumble.

But Gun glaring down at him had me quietly giggling.

"Shut up," Gun said.

Saint winked. "Take it out on me in the bedroom later—"

"Can you not announce your activities?" Lucas asked as he approached. "I don't want to hear what my brother and friend get up to."

"Lucas!" I cried. "My family is here." I shook Texas's shoulders again. "This is my brother, Texas. My mum, Low, and my dad, Dodge. Lucas belongs to Wreck."

"Holy fuck, you've gotta be into size kink," Mum blurted.

Laughter roared around us while Lucas blushed. Hell, even Wreck's lips twitched.

Mum winced. "Sorry, I can be inappropriate sometimes. I've got to remember we're not at home anymore."

"Now we know where Rommy gets it from," Saint teased.

I grinned. Mum had been in my life since I was seven, and Dad, who was actually our uncle, took us from New South Wales to live in Melbourne with him.

Mum and Dad were new at dating back then, but they were committed to each other. Not only did Dad take us on, but Mum too.

And since I'd been around her for so long, we were close, so of course I'd end up having some of her traits.

Dad snorted. "Welcome to my world. They're as bad as each other."

Mum and I grinned.

"Yet, you wouldn't have it any other way," Mum said. She stood and went to sit on his lap, curling into him. Dad placed his arm around her waist and kissed her temple.

"Fuckin' right."

This here was what I wanted.

Or even what Texas had with Maya.

Witnessing the love they held for each other in their gazes made me feel all warm and nice.

I stilled.

Had Texas announced about Maya?

While Dad chatted with Country, I leaned down and whispered in my brother's ear, "Before I got taken, did I guess right with Maya?"

Maya, having heard it, smiled up at me.

I gasped. "I did, didn't I? Have you told Mum and Dad?"

Texas sighed. "You did, but can you keep in contained for a bit longer? Now isn't the time. We need all families together."

I thinned my lips, but an excited *meep* escaped as I shook Texas's shoulders once again.

He reached up and tapped my hands. "You're givin' me whiplash."

I wrapped my arms around them both and hugged them tightly as I whispered, "Congrats. You guys will make great parents."

"What are you three plotting over there?" Mum asked.

I straightened and yelled, "Nothing!"

Laughter sounded around us, but my gaze landed on Quake, who was smirking and shaking his head at me.

Okay, I wasn't the best liar, and under pressure, I'd fold.

But I couldn't for this.

Even when I was bursting to shout it out, I wouldn't.

CHAPTER EIGHT

week later, I was walking inside from being with Dad and Saint, working on Saint's ride, and staring down at my phone when a text from Cal popped up. He was replying to one I'd sent hours ago, asking him why I was handling things differently than them.

They were still struggling to get through the ordeal—having sleepless nights or waking from horrid dreams—but I wasn't.

CAL:

Rommy, I'm saying this with love, but you're unique. I've never met anyone like you and I don't think I ever will. You were our rock on that boat. You were our sunshine, our hope. Everyone wanted to be around you because you were happy and positive all the time. Even those idiots who complained, they still listened to you, watched you, and wanted to be near you because you were our strength, our warmth. Honestly, I'm grateful this hasn't affected you like it has us because I doubt you could have been those things for us on that boat if you were any other way than you are. You're an inspiration and someone I want to call a friend for the rest of our lives. Thank you for everything you did for us and don't stress that you're not having nightmares. Talk soon!!!

Awww, that was so damn sweet it had my heart swelling. I loved when people took me for me and supported me as I was.

Yeah, I was glad I could stay positive, but I really did think it had a lot to do with my faith in my family. I knew without a doubt that we were going to be saved, and we were.

I'd just finished replying to him when I overheard Quake saying, "I haven't seen you in a long time."

There was a female snort. "There's a whole heap of club girls that'd keep you entertained."

"Eve, you know I don't sleep with them."

"Why don't you? I'm not stopping you."

"Maybe I want you to. Maybe I want you to care." He sighed. "Why are you avoidin' me?"

There was silence. I didn't think Eve was going to answer until I heard, "It doesn't matter."

"Don't you get it? I want you to trust me. To lean on me. Eve, I—"

"Just leave it," she snapped.

Quake said no more, but I heard his footsteps pounding away.

My chest ached for them both. I'd suspected there was something between them. Even a blind person could see the looks they tried to hide. Okay, probably not a blind person. But there was something stopping them. I didn't know what, though, but I figured they weren't sure either. Eve probably had an inkling, but I wasn't sure she was ready to face whatever it was holding her back.

When I heard a sniffle, I started to step forward but stopped.

I wasn't sure Eve would want me to see her upset. Since at the compound, I'd seen her in the background, watching, listening, but she was never close enough to interact with. I was confused why she kept her distance, but she was going to have to deal for now as I wasn't someone who stood around when someone was upset.

Drawing in a breath, I nodded to myself, determined to assist in some way. Even if it was so she could take her mood out on me.

Walking around the corner, I saw Eve's attention swing my way and her look of horror before I waved. "Hey, hi, hello, Eve. What's happening? I've just been working on the bikes with Saint and Dad. But I needed to come inside for some shade and to grab some drinks. You're not out with Mum, Courtney, Raya, and Dusty?"

Yes. I internally punched the air at remembering Courtney and Raya's name. Over the few days here, my parents and I had met just about everyone, and there were a lot to remember.

Eve's jaw clenched as she shook her head.

"Yeah, I like shopping, but not as much as Mum." I cocked my head to the side. "Are you okay?"

She glared. "Why?"

I shrugged. "You seem... more moody than usual. Not that there's anything wrong with being moody. We all have days where life shits down our throat. And anyway, you should see me on my period. No one wants to work close by my bay in the garage. I threw a screwdriver at Knife's head one day when he was teasing me." I laughed at the memory and then shrugged. "The shock on his face was priceless. Snapped me right out of my mood. Now the brothers just make sure there's chocolate bars stocked high in my cupboard and steer clear if they even think I'm on my peri-od." Leaning in, I mock whispered with my hand up to my mouth, "Sometimes I pretend to be grumpy, so they get me more chocolate." Straightening, I grinned.

The smile Eve gave me started small and then grew bigger. "You threw a screwdriver at a brother?"

"Ah yeah, he was teasing me about blushing over a customer we had and just wouldn't shut up. I shut him up. Now he doesn't tease me. Well, not as much. Most days I don't mind the guys and the shit they say, except—"

"When you're on your period," she said, still smiling.

I liked her smile. She was gorgeous already, but when she smiled it was like a shot of warm sun.

Huh, her and Quake's smiles make my body react.

Oh, shit, how hot would it be to see them together?

Crap, I couldn't think about that now, else I'd get hot and horny, and so far, I hadn't found anyone I wanted a roll in the sheets with. Well, besides Quake and Eve.

I tugged at the collar of my tee. "Exactly. What are you up to right now?"

Wanna hang out? I'd love to get to know you more. And maybe we could be friends before I work out how you'd respond to me sticking my tongue down your throat.

My gaze flicked down to her lips and up when she said, "I was going to see if Dusty was around to help me dye my hair, but you said she's out?"

I nodded and looked to the plastic bag in her hand. "What colour are you dying your hair? I can help. I'm more than happy to help. I've helped heaps of friends back home."

Eve looked down to the bag and back up. "Um, sure. As long as you have time."

I waved a hand. "Dad taught me everything I know; they'll be fine. But just wait one second, I need to grab them a drink and let them know I'll be back later."

"How about you go tell them, and I'll send a prospect out with drinks for them? I'll meet you in the common room?" she suggested.

I gave her two thumbs up. "Sounds like a plan." Clapping my hands together, I turned and walked back outside. "Guys, I'm going in to help Eve with something. A prospect will bring your drinks."

"No problem, kid," Dad said.

"Thanks, Rommy," Saint called.

On the way to the common room, I passed the prospect who was carrying a tray of assorted drinks. "Thanks, they're just around the corner from the front door."

He tipped his chin up at me.

When I stepped in the common room, I saw Eve waiting by the bottom of the stairs. I skipped up to her with a smile. "Ready."

Eve nodded and led me up the stairs. We went down some halls before we stopped in front of a door. "This is my room. Tech and I permanently live in the club."

Her tone sounded like she was worried what I'd think about it.

"That's cool."

Eve's shoulders dropped. She opened the door and moved in, stepping aside for me.

"Oh my God, it's a window seat." I walked right over to it. "I love window seats. I got Dad to put one in my room, but it's not as big as this." Looking out the window, I saw the back of the property where the trees overtook the land. "Sweet view."

"Thanks," Eve said.

Turning, I made my way over to her and picked up the bag she'd put on the bed. Peeking, I gasped and pulled out the box. "This colour is going to look awesome on you." Her blonde hair would soak up the red just nicely. Opening the box, I went to the door that led to the bathroom. "Should we do it in here?"

"Probably. I don't want red on the carpet."

"Ha, true. If I made a mess, it would look like you killed

someone." I looked around the spacious bathroom and said, "You'll need a chair."

I heard the wheels before she pushed one into the room. "Got it."

"Perfect. It says it works best on damp hair." I pulled the shower curtain back and grabbed the hose connected to one of the showerheads. I glanced back and tipped my head toward the shower. "Get over here."

Eve nodded before she grabbed a towel from the shelves that were embedded in the wall to place over her shoulders.

I started the water and made sure the temperature was perfect before I had her move closer.

"I can do this part myself," she said.

"I know" was all I said.

I wanted to do it for her, though.

She eyed me for a moment before moving up beside me and resting her hands on the edge of the bath to flick her hair over as she bent. I gently brushed my fingers through her soft locks at the base, making sure all strands were forward and then let the water flow over, darkening them to a medium blonde.

They weren't long, just past her shoulders, but Eve had a thick head of hair.

Once I shut off the water, I said, "All done. Towel dry it a bit and then I'll get to work."

I left her there and went to read the instructions again. They were pretty much the same as what we had in Australia. I was to part in sections, root to ends, use the gloves, mix the formulas, and start.

When Eve took a seat, I placed half of her hair up before breaking it into three where I tied two up.

Eve watched me in the mirror as I pulled on the gloves after I'd mixed it all together in the provided tub.

"This is the quietest you've been," Eve said.

Laughing, I shrugged. "Sometimes I can be. If I'm busy and my mind is on a task, like when I'm working or sexing it up with someone." I lifted my gaze to catch her blush. "But again, if I say anything you don't like, let me know. I won't get offended. I know I can be a bit much for some people."

Eve waved me off and kept her eyes on my hands as I worked in the colour with the brush. "It doesn't bother me. I guess... I guess people think that about me too. That I'm a bit much. Especially the club girls. They don't know how to take me."

"Why do you think that?"

"I'm not *girly* girly, and if they're being bitches, I tell them, which they don't like. I even deal out punishments if I have to. Like when they screw over the brothers or hurt one of my people."

"You're the alpha female. You have to keep a little distance from the club girls to make sure they do as they're told. It makes sense they tread carefully around you, and it's good to have that distance. I'm sure the brothers appreciate you being the one to deal with them when they step out. It's like that at home with Mum and the club girls. And I'm sure, like Mum, you have your own posse like Dusty, Courtney, Raya, and Wrenley who would help if asked, right? They'd do anything for you because you're their person. And they aren't the only ones who would help and enjoy your time and company and call you a friend. I've seen you with a lot of the other brothers."

She deadpanned. "I'm Tech's sister, and we've been here for a fucking long time."

I snorted. "And you think the connection with your brother will make them like you or hang with you? I'm Texas's sister, but we have our own little cliques. We both belong to the club and have been around since we were younger. You're in a place full of love and care. You belong here as much as Tech does."

I moved along to another part when she quietly said, "You said you've been around the club since you were younger. Not from birth?"

I shook my head. "Nah. Mum and Dad aren't our birth parents. Which I'm sure you've worked out since we look nothing alike."

She smirked. "I didn't want to presume."

"Fair enough. Dodge is our bio uncle. He took us in when I was seven and Texas was fourteen. Our mum passed away in a car accident."

"I'm sorry to hear that."

I gave her a tight smile and shook my head. "Believe me, Texas and I were better off with Uncle Trey. Huh, I haven't called him that in ages. When I was young, I asked if I could call him Dad and Low Mum, and they quickly agreed. We're their kids always and forever." Laughing lightly, I rolled my eyes. "Sorry, I got off track. Anyway, our bio mother didn't like us. Told us all the time. Screamed and ranted and pushed us. I knew Dad was the best kind of guy out there because he didn't even know us and yet he was willing to take care of us. He and Mum made it official soon after Dad brought us home."

When I met Eve's gaze in the mirror, her gaze was hard and her jaw clenched.

"Did I fuck up? Sorry if I said too much. I—" I snapped my lips closed and winced before I went back to finishing the final lower section.

"It's not you, Rommy."

I liked when she said my name.

"Parents?" I asked. "Not that you have to tell me. You hardly know me, and I get if—"

"Rommy." She laughed. "Breathe."

I took in a deep breath. "Sorry."

"Don't apologise." She sighed. "I just... I don't talk to anyone about it."

"No problem, babe. I'm going to start on the top part now." I undid her hair and then broke the strands into parts again before starting on the left.

Man, her hair was going to look amazing.

I bet Quake would... quake in his jeans. *Ha-ha.*

"Tech and I left the house to live on the streets," she said softly.

I didn't meet her gaze in the mirror in case she felt uncomfortable. Instead, I hummed and kept working on her hair.

She drew in a shuddering breath. "The streets were hell, but home life had been worse."

"Sucks when the ones who bring you into the world are the ones who treat you like crap."

"They hated each other and us just as much. Maybe they would have been... less toxic if they separated, but they didn't. They stayed together either high or drunk and cheated on each other. They were never shy about it either. Tech and I went without a lot. And their mood swings when they couldn't get high...." She shook her head. "The final straw was when the bitch wanted to get me high and pimp me out at sixteen."

I stilled, only moving my gaze up to see her hard one.

"Have they been taken care of?" I asked, my own voice like steel.

Her gaze widened. "What do you mean?"

I turned her in the chair around to face me and started at her hairline. "I presumed your club was like mine when it comes to dealing with our own situations. Like when Channa got noticed by some bad men after she helped my brother in a bad situation, so the club made sure she was protected. Turns out she's now married to a brother. Or when a club girl had to go home to see her father before he passed away, but the club knew she didn't like her home life, so a brother went with her. Ended up that brother now lives with the club girl's brother, and the club girl is an old lady to another brother. Huh, this probably sounds really confusing. Sorry. I'm getting to a point." I took a breath. "Then I heard about other times when people got kidnapped and the club rode in to rescue them while taking the law into their own hands and dealing out any punishment they saw fit." I sliced a thumb over my neck and dropped my head to the side while gagging. When I straightened, I finished the last spot at the hairline before I pinched her chin and drew her gaze up. "Have they been taken care of?" I asked again.

"No. We haven't seen them or wanted anything to do with them since the day we left."

"They're still breathing then."

She licked her dry lips and nodded.

I spun her chair back around and applied the last of the dye to her hair. "I hope they're suffering painfully in their hellhole that they created while you and your brother make the most out of the lives you have surrounded by people who love you both."

When I caught Eve's watery gaze, I silently cursed myself. Had I overstepped again?

"Sorry, I—"

She quickly reached up and grabbed my wrist, squeezing it. "Thank you." She sniffed and huffed out a laugh. "I don't know why I'm leaking. I... I just really appreciate your words —wishing the donors painful suffering." She snorted.

Grinning, I winked. "Any time." I stepped back and added, "Now you have to leave it in for half an hour." When Eve's phone rang, I busied myself with taking off the gloves and tidying up.

"Dusty, what's up? ... Tonight? ... I don't know ... Yeah, yeah. Okay ... I can let Rommy know. She's right here. ... Yep, later." She hung up and turned her chair around to face me. "The ladies want to go to Quake's bar tonight for drinks to celebrate Texas and Maya's last night. Also, apparently Henri needs a night out before he settles into his fathering role."

Laughing, I shrugged. "I'm in for sure. Did Dusty already tell Texas and Maya?" I gasped and clapped. "You'll get to show off your new hair."

She smiled. "She did. She's with them now. And let's hope it'll look okay."

"Babe, you could do anything to yourself, and you'd still look hot."

She blushed. "Ah, thanks?"

"No problem. Now, what's the best thing to wear to a place like Quake's bar?" Mum and Dad brought a heap of my clothes from home, as well as my phone, so I wanted to make sure I had the right thing to wear for this occasion. I also couldn't wait to see Quake's reaction to Eve's hair.

CHAPTER NINE

QUAKE

It was good to see the place was packed again. I smiled at a couple of regulars as I made my way through the tables to the bar. I'd just come back from the Polished Playground, the strip club I'd invested in with the brothers, to check on how things were coming along with the set-up and to make sure the booze order was correct.

I wasn't sure which place I'd be managing more at, but at least I had a second in charge I trusted to run things the way I did at both places.

"Drew, need any refills?" I called as I tapped the bar. I chuckled when he shot me the middle finger. Drew wasn't a member in the Diamond MC, but he was a guy who'd proved himself when I left him in the lurch the times I raced out the door to attend to club business. It was why I gave him a promotion over the other brothers who worked here since they'd be running out of the place with me if club business did arise.

Turning, I rested against the bar and looked around. There were two booths free that we could be putting people in.

"Drew, what—"

"Dusty called. She and her friends are coming in."

My damn gut fluttered.

That meant Eve, too, right?

And now there was a twist to my gut when I remembered Eve was avoiding me for some reason. She'd gotten something in her head that was stopping her from coming to me.

She still didn't understand it wasn't just about sex between us.

I wanted her as mine.

Even if Tech would beat me black and blue for touching his sister in the first place, I'd risk his wrath just to have her at my side all the time.

On the outside, she was tough and mouthy, but I'd seen a side to her that she hardly showed. A softer side that needed attention and affection and love.

Fuck me. I sounded like a smitten dick, but I couldn't help notice what Eve wanted, the love and affection, without her even saying it, and I wanted to be the one to give her everything she craved.

She didn't want to be in charge. She didn't want to be noticed or mouthy or mean.

She thought that was what people needed from her, so it was who she became.

In the bedroom, she mostly submitted to direction and

attention beautifully. Then there were days she was playful and needy.

But she was building her walls back up, which gutted me.

Her folks had screwed her and Tech in ways that'd cut deep. It was why she put on this hard exterior in the first place.

One I didn't think I'd ever crack.

Still, I really fucking wanted to try.

The door opened, and Dusty, Wrenley, Lucas, and West entered. My heart dropped to my gut when the door shut behind them. Until I perked up when it reopened. However, it was only Wreck, Adrick, and Torch.

She wasn't coming.

The women waved my way, and I tipped my chin to them and the others following.

I swung my gaze back to the door when it was pushed free again.

Eve stepped through with fiery red hair.

"Holy fuck," I muttered to myself. I loved her blonde, but this suited her so fucking much also.

She laughed from something someone behind her said as she moved to the side. The guy Texas, from Melbourne, walked in with his woman, Maya. I'd heard it was their last night with us. After them was Henri, Blaze, and Rommy, who skipped over to Eve and took her hand while smiling up at her and talking rapid-fire.

My damn breath caught in my throat over the soft expression on Eve as she listened to Rommy. When had these two connected in a way Eve gave her this look? I'd seen it a handful of times when she interacted with her friends, but

Rommy had somehow weaved her way under Eve's skin and infused more life into her and—

Eve threw her head back and laughed loudly as Rommy grinned big while watching her.

Christ. They were gorgeous together.

But I focused my attention on the woman I wanted as my own.

Eve rolled her eyes at Rommy, still smiling softly, and then Henri joined them by the door just before they started walking towards the booth.

"Boss, you're droolin'," Drew taunted.

Fuck, maybe I was. I wiped at my mouth and heard him chuckling.

Did I go over?

I wanted to see Eve up close. I wanted to talk to her and see if she changed her attitude when I was there.

Then again, the thought of her dimming made my chest ache.

Shit.

What the fuck should I do?

I took a step their way and stopped, turning back to the bar.

Drew's brows rose.

"Shut up," I told him.

"You gonna take their order?"

If I was here, I usually attended to the tables that held brothers and family so I could shoot the shit with them, but for the first time, I was hesitant.

Worry coursed through me.

"Boss?" Drew held out a tablet for me to take their order on.

Screw it.

I was going to do what I usually did.

And fucking pray my heart didn't break from seeing her face fall.

I snatched the device out of his hand and clipped, "Be back."

Drew smirked, but it quickly faded when he returned to filling drink orders.

As soon as I moved away from the bar, customers filled my spot. Luckily Drew wasn't the only one working. He had two others with him, and I always had another three employees on the floor taking orders, picking up empties, and cleaning down tables.

And I'm just trying to distract myself.

As I grew close, Rommy looked over and winked.

Snorting, I shook my head.

She'd made clear her attraction for me. It was refreshing and cute. She was funny. But I wouldn't give her the green light, as it would ruin any chance I had at making Eve mine.

I moved my gaze to Eve when I stopped beside their booth.

When her attention lifted to me, I held my damn breath and waited for her smile to vanish.

When it didn't, hope fucking flooded me.

"I like the hair," I told her.

She blinked, and a blush coated her cheeks. She lifted a hand to tuck some strands behind her ear. "Thanks. Rommy did it for me."

I nodded.

Say something else, you dickhead.
Tell her she's pretty.

No, you fucker, if you do that it'll put her walls up.

But she looks amazing tonight.

"This is a nice place, Quake," Rommy said, coming to the rescue. "Pick and Billy own a bar in Melbourne that I always go to. I think it's good to have a safe space like this owned by the club. But Henri was telling me about the strip club opening up." She got to her knees on the seat. "That's so exciting. I'm not sure I'll be around to see it open, though." She turned to Henri. "When will it open?"

"We are hoping to open in a month, chéri."

She screwed up her nose. "Damn, I doubt the parents want to stay that long."

"Doesn't mean you can't," Eve suggested, and Dusty nodded from the other side of Eve.

Rommy moved on her knees to face Eve next to her. "Huh?"

Eve smiled. "Your parents might go back, but you could stay a bit longer."

Rommy slapped the table to get her brother's attention. "Do you think I could? Would it work? I've never been to a strip club. I want to see this one on opening day."

Texas smirked. "Rom, you're old enough to make up your own mind. But if we all left you here, we'd need someone to travel back to Australia with you for safety."

She was already nodding. "I know. I get it. Dad would lock me away if he could, so I'll do anything to ease his stress."

"Where are your parents tonight, chéri?" Henri asked from where he was leaning into Blaze.

"They stayed at the compound. You'll have to drop in one day soon to meet them. They'll love you." She gasped.

"Oh my God, do you know who else will love you. Julian—"

"No," Blaze bit out.

Any other person would have taken the warning in his tone and shut up, but Rommy laughed and shook her head. "Relax, big man. Julian has his own beau. I'm just saying they'd be friends. He's Maya's uncle."

"I think if they ever met, that Blaze and Uncle Mattie would turn grey from all the trouble they'd conjure up," Maya said.

Henri grinned. "Oh, chéri, I would love to meet this man."

"Quake," Wrenley called from the booth over where she sat with Torch, Adrick, West, Lucas, and Wreck. "Can we order, please?"

"You got it." I moved to their table. Adrick complained that I didn't have any Russian beer, but West quickly scolded his husband. "I'll get some another time," I told him.

He nodded once. "*Da*, do that. I would come here more often and bring my guards."

Lucas snorted. "Like you would go anywhere without West."

Adrick stared at him. "I did not say I wouldn't have West with me."

Lucas rolled his eyes. "Of course."

I finished taking their orders and sent them off to the bar and kitchen before moving back to the other table. A table where I wanted to sit if I wasn't working.

"What's everyone interested in tonight?"

"Rom," Texas warned quickly, and I caught her snapping her lips closed before smirking.

"Can I have some chips and aioli, please," Maya asked.

"Chips? What kind?"

"Fries," Rommy shouted. "She means fries. And I'll get some hot wings. We'll share a jug of soda too."

"Not drinking tonight?" I asked her.

Texas huffed. "She doesn't need alcohol."

Rommy squirmed on the seat. "That's right. I'm the life of a party no matter."

"I believe that," Dusty said. "I'll grab a gin and tonic since I pumped enough milk that it won't bother Seth. No food. I had an early dinner before I left home."

Texas, Blaze, and Henri ordered drinks too. Then I turned to Eve.

"What would you like?"

Me?

I'd offer myself up so fucking fast.

The growl in her stomach was loud enough to be heard over the music. "Vodka and orange juice, thanks."

"No food?"

She shook her head.

"Let's grab another bowl of fries and wings. We'll all share?" Rommy suggested. I liked that she wanted to take care of Eve, too, and I bet she could convince Eve to eat as well.

"You got it," I said, tapping at the screen. "Shouldn't be too long."

"Thanks, Quake," Rommy offered.

I tipped my chin up at her before I headed back over to the bar. I stepped behind it this time and started serving.

It was a ploy to keep busy so I wouldn't just stand and stare back at the table.

"I'm surprised you didn't stay," Drew commented in passing.

I wanted to.

I wished I had.

But I also didn't want to be the reason Eve's night went sour. I had a feeling if I stuck around, I'd do or say something that'd annoy her.

I tended to do that a lot, but at least in the few years we'd been sleeping together, I was able to work out what I did and fix it.

Only this time, I didn't have a clue what was wrong, and she wasn't opening up to me.

Maybe Rommy could find out.

But that'd be a sneaky dick move if I asked Rommy to help.

I'd just taken the money from another customer when I moved my attention to the booth. The food and drinks had arrived. I knew the drinks had because I helped make them while one of my servers took them over, but I hadn't seen one of the waitstaff take the food out.

Rommy was still kneeling on the seat, half leaning over the table while talking up a storm. She had her hand on Eve's shoulder, and Eve watched the other woman with humour in her gaze.

The women and Henri laughed at something Rommy said.

I hadn't seen Eve so relaxed in a long time. She could get that way in the bedroom or around her inner circle, but tonight was different again. It was like something had been lifted off her shoulders, and I had a feeling it was something Rommy did.

Rommy picked up a wing and passed it to Eve even while she was talking to her brother on the other side of the table.

Eve studied the wing and then glanced to Rommy, her face softening before she took a bite.

My cock twitched in my jeans.

She was stunning normally, but there was something extraordinary seeing her this at ease.

It was like she glowed.

How did I get her to do that for me?

I'd managed to give her something similar when we'd been together in bed. But as soon as she thought she had to get out of there, she locked up her real self and hardened once more.

Christ, I wanted her like this all the time.

Not for me. Not for anyone else but herself.

She deserved this all the time instead of being stuck in her head.

Maybe I needed to kidnap Rommy so she could always bring that carefree, happy, and wide smile to Eve's lips.

CHAPTER TEN

EVE

*R*ommy stood beside the booth and reached down for my hand while begging, "*Please*. Please come dance."

I snorted. "No one is dancing, Rommy."

Dusty, who was now drunk, shoved at my side. "We'll make our own dance floor. Let's do this."

Henri perked up from leaning against Blaze's chest and clapped. "Oui. I want to dance. Let me out, please. I need to connect my music to the speakers."

"I don't think Quake will let you," West said. He and Adrick had drifted to our table when Texas and Maya moved to the other. We'd been swapping all night, getting to know the Australians.

"You should ask. Everyone thinks you are the prettiest," Henri suggested.

"No, he's not," Blaze said.

"He is." Adrick glared.

Blaze's jaw clenched. "Henri is."

"Aww, mon amour, you are so getting rewarded for that later." He leaned back and kissed Blaze's jaw. But Blaze was too busy glowering at Adrick, who was doing the same back.

Rommy wiggled my arm. "Come on, come on. Let the guys piss over their men while we get our groove on."

I needed more drinks for this.

Still, I couldn't say no when she looked so damn excited.

Sighing, I moved out of the booth, and Dusty bumped into my back when she practically flew up and over to the only clear spot on the floor. She threw her arms in the air and started swaying while Wrenley joined her.

Before Rommy could drag me over, my wrist was seized by Henri. "I am stealing her for a moment, chéri. You can come too. We will go seek out Quake. There is a song I wished played for my amour."

"Let's do this," Rommy said, and they dragged me over to the bar. I glanced back to see Lucas joining the other two while Torch and Wreck stood guard to scowl at anyone close.

"Quake," Henri called, and my blood rushed through my veins.

I looked to where he was serving someone to see him hold up a finger.

"He is looking very well tonight," Henri commented.

I caught him and Rommy sharing a look.

"I reckon he's the hottest brother," Rommy said.

He was.

Which was why it was so easy to fall into bed with him. He was the kind, funny, and swoon-worthy handsome.

And I'm just a bitch to him.

My smile vanished, and I dropped my gaze to the floor.

He couldn't want me like he thought he did.

People ended up cheating in the end anyway. I was just saving myself from heartache.

No one would want me long term.

I didn't—

Rommy's hand in mine squeezed before her face appeared in front of mine. "Do you know I used to think that all guy's dicks were circumcised?"

I blinked and lifted my head. What in the world was she talking about?

She nodded. "I accidently saw my dad's dick. I was nine, and my parents thought they were home alone. Well, they were, but I was just next door you see, and I wanted to show Mena my new Monster High doll, so I just raced home. They were naked in the kitchen when I walked in. I saw his dick, so I thought all others were like his. Until I was about to get my freak on with a guy who wasn't circumcised. I was fascinated by it. I kept wanting it to deflate so I could see it get covered again. Like a turtle popping his head out."

An abrupt laugh escaped me.

"Chéri, you are a true treasure, and don't let anyone tell you otherwise," Henri told Rommy, and I completely agreed.

She'd gotten me out of my head. Saved me from spiralling down that dark path.

I wanted to hug her for it.

And for me that was big because I didn't like too much affection.

Yet, for Rommy....

Releasing her hand, I curled my arms around her shoulders and dragged her against me to hold on tightly.

Please don't push me away.

Please let me hold you.

Please.

Too many times I'd thought no one would want me close to them. No one would want me to touch them. Too many times I'd been told I was ugly, useless, and disgusting. That I'd end up alone and miserable because no one could stand me.

Words after words bombarded my mind, mixing me up, messing me up where it was just easier to believe them.

When her arms wrapped around my waist, the tension rolled off my body, and I drew in a deep breath. She smelled of something fruity. Sweet, like she was.

Against my chest, she said, "Not that I mind having my face pressed against your breasts, but I'm having a major lady boner right now, and my hand doesn't want to listen to my mind when I tell it I can't grab your boob."

Heat hit my face.

Still, she had me laughing and relaxing as we released each other.

I took her hand and mouthed, "Thank you."

She winked.

Henri tapped the bar with his knuckles, gaining our attention so he could ask Rommy, "Chéri, are you into women?"

Rommy shrugged. "I love love. If they're a guy or a girl or whoever they want to be... if I feel the attraction, I'm willing to explore. I want my happy ever after like Mum and Dad or Texas and Maya. I'm surrounded by love at home, and I know that one day I'll find my person or people to live the rest of my life with."

She was the most positive person I'd ever met.

I wasn't sure anything could get her down. Hell, she'd been kidnapped and walked out fighting.

I loved her look on life and love.

In a mere matter of moments alone with her in my room, I felt like I could trust her, like I wanted to stick close and soak up her sunshine.

"That is a beautiful thing, chéri. And to know this at such a young age."

I nodded. "Henri's right."

"Like always," Henri added.

Snorting, I rolled my eyes. "I wouldn't say always, but on this, yes. I'm twenty-seven, and I still don't know what I want."

"You will work it out, chéri."

"Hey."

I jumped at Quake's voice.

"Sorry," he said to me. I waved him off. "What can I get you three?"

"Music," Rommy said.

Quake's brows pinched. "Sorry?"

"I am hoping you will allow me to connect to your music because there is a song I wish to play for mon amour." Henri pressed his hands together under his chin. "Pretty please?"

Quake looked at all of us slowly, his gaze lingering on me for that little bit longer, which was why Henri had brought me over.

Quake sighed. "One song. Tell me what it is, and I'll add it to the playlist."

Henri squealed and gave Quake the song title and singer. It wasn't even a song I'd heard of.

"Merci," Henri shouted before blowing him a kiss. With that, we went to the dance floor.

Like the others in our group, Rommy had rhythm. She moved to the music in a sensual sway, but I was never the best dancer. I enjoyed doing it, but I became too self-conscious. Especially here, knowing Quake was around.

"I'm going to get a drink," I called to the others.

"Come back after," Rommy said.

I wouldn't, but she didn't need to know that. I went over to the booth and sat with the others.

"Not in the mood to dance?" Maya asked.

"I need to be drunker for it."

She laughed. "I totally understand."

"I'm going out there," West announced.

"*Nyet*," Adrick clipped, and I didn't think he meant to because he froze.

"Did you say no to me?" West demanded.

"*Da?*"

I covered my mouth to hide my big grin. The uncertainty in the big scary guy's tone was hilarious.

"Adrick—"

"We will go together is what I meant."

West beamed. "Sounds perfect." They slipped out of the booth, and West dragged Adrick over near the others.

There was a song change and then Henri squealed. Surprise filtered through me at his song choice. "Something to Feel" by Dallas Dixon was a country song. Not at all what I expected. Henri pointed at Blaze and winked.

But then I heard the words.

My eyes widened from the song, which was about sexual desire for a guy and absolutely unapologetic for it, as well as the way Henri moved his hips as he danced closer to the table.

Looking to the bar, I laughed at seeing Quake with his head tipped back, looking to the ceiling. Like he was praying for guidance or for someone to take him from this world.

"What the fuck is this shit?" a voice boomed.

My attention swung to the guy storming the dance floor, his hand wrapped around Henri's arm, and the table in front of me disappeared with a loud crack, making Maya and I scream in surprise.

The top of the table dropped with another loud bang to the floor. I jolted and briefly thought that Blaze could have asked us to move, but this big, fierce man was already standing and rushing towards Henri. But then Rommy was already there. As Adrick protected West, and Torch with Wreck got Lucas, Dusty, and Wrenley out of the way, Rommy jumped on the guy's back who was shaking Henri and yelling in his face. As soon as her arm locked around the guy's neck, he released Henri to try and peel her away, but she held strong.

"Shit," Texas shouted. He stood and started for the commotion, but Blaze had already arrived. He reached out, and Rommy took Blaze's hand before she jumped down and got out of the way just as Blaze reared his arm back and let his fist fly into the guy's face.

The guy dropped and didn't get up again.

A woman screamed and started running over.

The music cut off, and Quake roared, "Enough." He clicked his fingers and other brothers appeared. One grabbed the woman, while another two lifted the guy off the floor. "Don't come back," Quake ordered as the brothers escorted the idiots out. Quake banged his fist against the bar. "And if anyone else thinks they can start shit like that, you can get the fuck out of my place." He strode out from behind the bar and over to the dance floor.

Henri met him. "I am so sorry. I—"

Quake's hand landed on his shoulder, and he patted him twice before he dropped it. "You did nothin' wrong. The song was funny as fuck."

"Are you sure?"

"Henri, relax, yeah? It's on those fuckwits." He looked over Henri's head to where Blaze stood with his hands clenched at each side. The guy was breathing heavily. His face screamed that he wanted to continue hurting that dickhead for touching Henri. "Blaze," Quake called. Blaze's gaze snapped his way. "Come reassure your man that this wasn't on him, yeah?"

"That was fun," Rommy said as she stepped up beside me with her brother. I stood with them.

Texas ruffled her hair. "Rom, you've got to reevaluate what fun means."

"Teaching someone not to be a dick is fun, bro."

Texas shook his head while Maya and I laughed.

"What happened here?" Rommy asked, staring down at the broken wood from the missing table.

"Blaze just pushed it out of the way," Maya said with awe in her tone. She stood and went to her husband, who curled her into his side with a kiss to the top of her head. He whispered something that had Maya tipping her head back and smiling softly up at him.

My heart ached.

I wanted that, but I couldn't have it.

Rommy rubbed her hands together. "Man, I'd love to fight Blaze."

"Don't even fuckin' think of askin'," Texas demanded.

Rommy cackled.

Quake appeared and stopped in front of Rommy and me, his gaze locked on mine. "Are you okay?"

His concern made my belly flutter, but I rolled my eyes and snorted. "I wasn't even involved."

My tone was cold.

I hated myself when I saw his subtle flinch.

His jaw clenched and he moved his gaze to Rommy. "Nice moves."

She grinned. "Thanks. I have many more moves." She wiggled her brows.

The innuendo was clear. She wanted to show him her moves, and he was better off with her than the likes of me, who couldn't give him what he deserved or what he wanted: a nice happy family.

My head was too messed up.

He'd have enough of me in the end and leave.

Quake said something else to Rommy who replied, but I didn't hear anything but the ringing in my ears. My mind jumbled.

She'd be perfect for Quake.

I could see them together with a bunch of kids in a cute home where she'd take care of the garden with him.

They worked.

He should just go for her.

"Eve?" Quake said, and I was sure it wasn't the first time since everyone was looking at me.

"What?" I snapped.

Fuck. I was a bitch. I hated this. I hated hurting him. But I couldn't stop myself.

"Uh-oh, someone needs to get to bed," Rommy sang. She took my hand, and I allowed it, staring down at her soft hand in mine.

I didn't like affection. I wasn't used to it, and my skin crawled. Yet, it didn't do that with Rommy, and it never did when Quake and I were in bed.

I'd hugged my friends a handful of times, and when I did, I wanted out of their embrace as soon as it started. It was never because of them, but me and my stupid head.

Why couldn't I just accept touch or compliments?

Because you don't deserve them. No one will put up with you. You're nothing.

Rommy lifted our joined hands up to wrap her other one around both of ours and tuck them against her shoulder. "Don't worry, big guy. I'll make sure she gets to bed and is well rested for a nice and pleasant conversation in the morning."

No. There wouldn't be a conversation.

He needed to forget about me.

Even when the thought of not seeing him again was like a gunshot to the chest, leaving me open and broken.

Jesus, I was screwed.

CHAPTER ELEVEN

When I walked Eve to her room last night, it seemed like her thoughts were getting the better of her because of how silent she'd become. I couldn't say for sure what was bothering her, but something had her distant—like she couldn't bring herself to be close to the man she loved.

I'd noticed it at the bar, too, which was why I'd tried to take her mind off things. But on the drive to the compound, whatever it was kept pulling her under, and I couldn't reach her.

Did other people see her struggles?

Did she let them?

I was surprised she opened up to me about her heartbreaking past.

It really boiled my blood when kids had to deal with parents like that.

No, it did more than that. I wanted to hunt them down and destroy them.

I am my father's daughter.

Eve suffered on the inside. I could tell. If she didn't, I was certain she'd be locked in a relationship with that gorgeous man.

Whatever her parents poisoned her with—words and actions—she was still letting that fester and control her now.

It wasn't right.

But what could I do?

Be there for her.

Of course I would. She was someone special. I just knew it.

Slowing my steps, I cut off my train of thought and took a deep breath as I stretched my arms and legs. I'd just finished running the perimeter of the compound for the tenth time, and if I didn't get food in my stomach soon, it wasn't going to forgive me.

I walked into the kitchen from outside. "Hey, hi, hello," I called to Chaos, Rule, Saint, Gun, and Boomer.

I was pretty proud of myself for remembering all their names. What helped was when I remembered something specific about them. Like Chaos with his wild long hair. Rule was young and had a tattoo of a snake winding around his arm from his wrist to up under his tee. Saint and Gun were easy because I'd met them on the first day here and we'd talked for hours about bikes. Boomer was another easy name to remember because he actually talked loudly.

"Morning, kid," Boomer boomed.

I got chin lifts from Rule and Gun, while Saint winked. Chaos wouldn't look at me, though.

"What's wrong, Chaos?" I asked.

Chaos said, "Darlin', if my old lady caught me lookin' at you, a single, new woman who isn't one of the club women... one she knows I've nothin' to do with, she'd nail my nuts to the floor."

I glanced down at myself. Brows pinched in confusion. I lifted my gaze just when the kitchen doors opened and Quake strolled in as I said, "But I'm not naked. My boobs and vagina are covered."

Chaos made a pained sound while the others chuckled.

"Sorry. But I'm saving my nuts. My woman is a crazy one. Not that I'd have her any other way, but I like to stay unharmed," Chaos said before he walked out with a smirking Rule following.

I really didn't get it. I had on a sports bra and boy shorts. I glanced down again and cupped my breasts, pushing them up. "There's not even cleavage."

"Jesus, kid. Quit it," Boomer called. Then he huffed. "Reminds me of the time when Gun found out what he could do with his pecker."

"Fuckin' hell, Boomer. Shut your trap, old man."

The other men chuckled.

I shrugged and walked to the counter to steal a raspberry muffin. I took a bite and moaned around the goodness.

"We're headin' out to the tables. You comin', Rommy?" Saint asked.

"I'm gonna grab some more food first. Be out soon." I went over to grab a plate.

"Meet you out there," Gun said as he, Saint, and Boomer left.

Now I was alone with Quake.

The handsomest man in the club whose peen I really wanted to see.

A shame he was off limits.

But the real question was should I keep my mouth shut and not get involved with him and Eve, or would it be helpful if I did say something?

Shit. What should I do?

I couldn't say anything, could I?

It really wasn't my place.

But Eve... she needed a slight helping hand, right?

Turning, I found Quake already staring at me from where he leaned against the counter with his arms crossed.

He smirked. "I could hear you thinking."

Smiling, I brought my plate over to the counter and started piling on food. "Dad always says he can see the wheels turning before I start to speak." Laughing lightly, I shrugged. "At least whoever I'm going to talk to can prepare themselves."

"Is what you're going to say bad?" he asked as he went to pick up a plate too.

Placing my dish down, I shook my head. "No, no. Not bad." How did I say this? What was I going to say? "I-I, hell, I don't want to put my foot in it, but I think you need to know that Eve does like you. Anyone can read it. I think she's a bit in love with you, but she has struggles. I won't say what. That's for her to tell you."

"About her parents?"

"Yes. Has she told you anything?"

He shook his head. "Not really, and neither has Tech. They're both tight-lipped about it, but I've gathered being around their parents was a shitty time for them."

"It plays on her mind a lot, and I think adds to her... not being herself, if that makes sense? I've heard some of the club girls talk about Eve, and they're all scared of her. I know she takes care of matters for the brothers when it comes to the women, but I don't think that's who she really wants to be. Oh my God, I probably shouldn't be saying any of this. I suck. I'm not a good friend at all, but I hate seeing her struggle. And it seems I can't shut up either. Please ignore everything I've just said. She'll kill me for this."

I buried my face in my hands.

It was wrong. I made the wrong choice and now—

"Do you know you bring out a side to her that she keeps close to her heart? A side I've only seen glimpses of."

Dropping my hands, I cocked my head to the side. "Huh?"

He chuckled.

God, that sounded nice. Like Eve's laugh did.

It was such a pity that neither of them looked at me with heat in their eyes.

It actually made my heart hurt.

But I couldn't be too upset because they were so into each other, and I loved that for them.

"Last night Eve was... Christ, this is gonna sound weird, but it was like she glowed when she was around you. Like you made everything bad disappear and had her smiling and laughing as if she didn't have a care in the world."

I waved him off. "She's like that with her posse."

His brows rose, and amusement shone in his gaze. "Posse?"

"Oh, Julian always calls the old ladies of the club the pussy posse."

His laugh was loud, and my grin was instant.

"I get it." But the look he gave me made me think he wished he didn't get it. "And in a way, you're right about Eve with her *posse*. Although, I think, even with them that she's kept them at a distance. Not you, though."

"I'm easy to talk to," I offered.

For the first time, his gaze swept over my body, but he did it so quickly I nearly missed it before he was eyeing the food. "I won't give up on her,' he said quietly.

And that was exactly what I wanted.

Beaming, I clapped. "Perfect."

He studied me and scrubbed a hand over his head. "You really think she loves me?"

"Without a doubt. But it's hidden deep, and she's scared — Fuck. I shouldn't have said that. Ignore what I said. I can hit you over the head to give you a concussion and hopefully amnesia. Just a short case of it to forget this moment."

Another chuckle rolled out of him, this one low and rough. "Forget about what?"

"That I said.... Wait, I see what you're doing." I shot him fingers guns. "You're a cool, big guy, Quake, and if I wasn't rooting for you and Eve, I would have so tried to get in your pants."

He coughed and spluttered and went beet red.

Cackling, I picked up my plate again and winked. "Good luck," I said before I walked out into the common room.

There was a spot left on the table that held my parents,

Texas, Maya, Saint, Gun, and Boomer. When I got to the table, I kissed Dad and Mum on the cheek before hugging Texas and Maya with one arm since I still held my plate of food.

"Mornin', girl," Mum said. "You been out for a run?"

"Yep, just around the compound."

"You wore that?" Dad demanded. "Go and get a tee on or a damn body-length turtleneck."

The men chuckled.

I rolled my eyes as I sat down. "The ladies aren't peeking out. If I've offended anyone with what I'm wearing, please tell me and I'll go get into something else."

"You're offendin' my eyes," Texas said. Maya slapped him in the side.

"You don't count," I told my brother. However, I doubted anyone would actually tell me I was making them uncomfortable, and I should consider the old ladies of the club. They may not want to see me dressed like this around their guys.

I took a large mouthful of the eggs and stood. "I'll be back. Mind my spot, please."

Mum winked at me. She was happy that I gathered it wasn't just about me and that I had to think of others. Sometimes I could forget that. To me, a body, no matter what shape or size, was a beautiful thing to showcase, but not everyone thought like I did.

Laughing to myself as I climbed the stairs, I was sure no one thought like me.

I was walking down the hall when I caught sight of Eve.

"Hey, hi, hello," I called and then skipped down to her. When I was at her side, I wrapped my arms around her waist. She stiffened for a moment before hugging me back.

"Morning. Have you already had breakfast?"

I pulled back. "I have a plate ready down there, but I wanted to grab a sweater."

"I'll come with you." When we started walking, I could tell she wanted to say something from the way she kept parting and closing her lips. I waited it out, even when I wanted to ask how she was or to see what her plans were for the day. Maybe I could convince her to play some video games with me in Quake's room.

Oh, oh, oh. I really wanted to take another look at Quake's bed. Did they have sex there or in Eve's room? I'd been in both, but I hadn't studied them like I now wanted to.

God, they would really be a sight together.

Eve was taller than me, but Quake still towered over her.

Imagine their bodies sliding and grinding together on the sheets.

Hot. Hot. Hot. Hot.

"I'm sorry about last night," she said softly as we entered the room I slept in.

"What for? I thought it was a good night. I had fun. I mean, I'd like to have punched that guy myself, but that's okay. What kind of fool gets upset from a song like that?" At the drawers, I removed a thin sweater. I yanked it over my head and put my arms in while saying, "I came back to my room last night and listened to some more Dallas Dixon songs. I think they're awesome. Some are really funny, but his voice is perfect for the songs."

"Rommy."

Turning to her, I saw she was wringing her hands together. "What's wrong?" I asked.

She let out a watery huff. "I'm trying to figure out what it is about you that makes me want to tell you things that I've never told anyone else. Why I feel like I can tell you that I'm tired of putting on this hard, strong front all the time. I don't mind it when someone needs me to deal with the women of the club because sometimes they do things that really piss me off, and they deserve to be taught a lesson, but I'm...." She threw up her arms and turned away.

"I think there comes a time in life when you just get to the point when enough is enough. You don't have to take the weight of the world on your shoulders. You can lean on people who want to help you, who want nothing more but for you to be who you want to be. If there's an issue with the women and you're not interested in dealing with it, someone else will. No one would want you to do anything you don't want to."

"I beat up a woman who was connected to Dusty being kidnapped. At the time, it felt good. I wanted to see her pain and fear. But... even to this day when I look at my hands sometimes I see her blood, and it crushes me. I realised I'm not made out for that type of punishment. A slap to the face to knock some sense, yes, but not that."

"Then don't. No one will care, Eve. In the days I've been here, I see so much love and support for everyone. It reminds me so much of home, and I know that if I didn't want to hurt someone, even when they deserve it, then I wouldn't have to. Someone is always at my back to help me."

She let out a small, strained laugh. "Maybe this was why

I kept my distance from you. You make too much sense. You're too nice and sweet and tough."

"Stop, you're making me blush," I teased.

She turned and smiled. "For days I watched every person you talk to fall in love with you. I'm not talking about in a sexual way. Well, some of the brothers maybe. But you have this ease about you that makes people want to be around you."

The sweetness of her words made me all melty on the inside.

"You know you're the same. People search you out to be around you. And there's a certain someone who is completely—"

She paled. "Don't please."

Reaching out, I took her hand and led her to the bed to sit down beside me. "Why?"

She sighed and then shrugged. "Quake is... he's too much for me."

I jerked my head back. "How?"

"He's perfect, sweet, sexy, considerate, smart... everything I'm not. He deserves someone—"

I gently slapped her forearm. "I'm going to stop you right there."

She snorted. "Okay."

"He doesn't want anyone else." When she went to say something, I pressed a finger to her perfect, pretty lips, making her glare. I smiled before I dropped my hand and said, "I've seen the way he looks at you, and it's easy to see how amazing he thinks you are. He wants to make you his. So maybe try to stop letting whatever your parents said and did blind you from something that—"

"But—"

"Nope. How long have you and Quake been sleeping with each other?"

"Years."

"Babe," I whispered. "I'd bet my left tit that neither you nor he has slept with anyone else in that time."

"I haven't. I don't know about him."

Cupping her cheeks, I squished them together. "Eve, babe. Quake is your man. It's time you make an honest man out of him."

She snorted again. "My brother—"

"Probably already knows. People aren't oblivious to you and Quake."

"But—"

"Do you love him?"

We stared at each other, and her tears welled before she nodded.

"Then take what your heart wants and enjoy the lives you can build together because I already believe it could be something outstanding."

She sniffed. "You're a bitch."

Grinning, I released her cheeks and stood. "Only when I'm making you see how worthy you are."

"I'm n—"

"You are, and I won't hear any more of it."

There was a knock against the wall before Tech peeked his head around.

"Hey, hi, hello," I greeted.

He smiled. "Mornin', Rommy. Your brother and Maya are heading off shortly. He sent me up here to grab you." His gaze slid to his sister, face tightening. "What's goin' on?"

Turning to Eve, I raised my brows. As far as I was concerned, it was the best time to tell her brother about her and Quake. Ideally before she chickened out and her thoughts got the better of her. I'd happily drag her back to reality about how awesome she was.

Eve drew in a deep breath and said, "Quake and I are something."

I smiled proudly at her before I looked back to Tech... and wondered why he grinned evilly.

CHAPTER TWELVE

QUAKE

My gaze kept swinging to the plate Rommy had left behind. Saint had told me it was hers, but she'd gone upstairs a while ago. What was she doing that kept her up there? Her food would go to waste, and she seemed like the kind of woman who would be annoyed if she didn't get to finish a meal. She loved food just about as much as I did.

Hell, she probably loved it more based on her moans.

She'd surprised me earlier, and not about wanting to sleep with me if Eve wasn't in the picture. It was because she'd, in her roundabout way, told me to not give up with Eve.

Could that mean they'd talked?

Did I have a chance to make Eve mine?

Christ, my gut fluttered at the thought.

Texas and Maya stopped by the table. Texas tipped his chin up. "Mornin'."

"Are you two sure you don't want me to come to the airport?" Low asked.

"We'll be—"

"Tech, wait" was yelled, and we all turned towards the stairs to see Tech striding down them with Eve and Rommy following. Rommy was grinning, but Eve looked panicked.

I stood as they got closer. "What's goin' on?"

"Tech, don't—"

My brother stopped in front of me, pulled his arm back, and punched me in the face.

"Tech!" Eve snapped.

I turned to Tech, who was up in my face. "Been itchin' to do that for some fuckin' time."

"Why?" I asked hesitantly, glancing to Eve and back. My cheek stung like a bitch, but I ignored it.

She wouldn't have said anything, right?

If she did... fuck me, but I'd be damn thrilled.

"Why?" Tech clipped. "You and my sister, ring any bells?"

I shot my wide gaze to Eve. "You told him?" I asked, smiling wide.

She rolled her eyes but blushed as she shrugged.

"Eve?" I pressed.

"I'm not done talkin' to you," Tech bit out.

"Eve?" I asked again, my gaze glued to her. When she nodded, my goddamn heart took off out of my chest and flew high.

Tech groaned. "Jesus, brother."

Ignoring him, I moved over to Eve and cupped her cheeks. "What does this mean, sweetheart?"

"Now he straight up ignores me," Tech complained.

Eve reached up and touched my cheek. "Sorry, my idiot brother—"

"I don't care. I'll take all the hits from him." I needed to know. "Eve, why did you tell him?"

She flicked her gaze off to the side where I noticed Rommy stood with her hands clasped under her chin watching us with happiness. She winked and nodded at Eve.

Fuck me.

Fuck me.

Fuck me.

What had Rommy said to have Eve telling her brother and my best fucking friend in the club that we're something?

Was Eve ready to commit?

Did she honestly want me?

When Eve looked back up at me, she said, "I want to try." Her bottom lip trembled. She bit down on it until I brushed my thumb over the plump flesh, and she released it.

"You're mine?"

"It's not going to be easy," she warned.

"You're mine?"

"Quake, I'm messed up, and I could say things that—"

Leaning down, I kissed her, and against her lips, I smiled before mumbling, "You *are* mine."

"Yes," she whispered and then wrapped her arms around my neck right before I claimed my woman with a kiss in front of everyone.

Cheers, catcalls, and clapping bombarded our ears. For a

split second, I worried Eve would pull away and run, but she didn't. She held me tighter and kissed me deeper.

Fucking hell.

This was Eve in my arms in front of everyone.

Eve.

The woman I'd wanted to claim since the first night we'd slept together. It may have been a drunken romp then, but I'd woken up and watched her sleep peacefully next to me for half an hour knowing that she was gonna mean something to me.

And she does.

She was mine, and I wouldn't let her get away from me now.

No matter what.

"Christ, all right, enough sucking my sister's face," Tech barked.

Laughter sounded as I kissed Eve one more time before pulling away and grinning like a crazy guy down at her. My chest swelled when she smiled just as brightly up at me.

Turning to Tech, I asked, "You want to hit me again?"

He'd been studying his sister with a clenched jaw, but then he looked at me. "I do, but I know she'd get pissed if I did."

"I would," Eve said.

Tech glared at me with his arms crossed over his chest. "She deserves the world."

"I'll give it to her," I told him honestly.

Eve shook her head. "I... no... I don't—"

Rommy clapped her hands. "So sorry to interrupt. Tech, you can get back to threatening Quake later. But my brother's about to go, and we all need to say goodbye."

Texas dropped his head back and sighed. "We could have just snuck out."

"No, we can't," Maya said, nudging him.

I curled Eve under my arm and held her tightly to my side.

I could do that now.

She was mine.

I could hold her, talk to her in front of people, and show everyone she was under my care.

Christ. I couldn't keep the smile from my mouth even if I wanted to.

Texas grinned. "Right. Dodge, Low. There was somethin' we wanted to share before we leave."

"What?" Low asked, perking up.

Texas held Maya to him, his grin growing even more. Like he was proud about something. Then he announced, "I'm fuckin' thrilled to let you know, Maya's pregnant."

Low stood screaming. She danced around on the spot, then rushed them.

Rommy cackled and skipped over to them too. "I'm going to be the best aunty," she announced. "I'll take him or her or whatever they want to be to get their first piercing and tattoo and drinks and—"

Texas pulled her in for a hug. "No, you won't." He then told his wife, "Our kid ain't stayin' with my sister."

Maya, who was tucked under a crying Low's arm, gave her husband a watery smile. "We'll see."

"Ha," Rommy cried. "That means yes they can."

As Dodge congratulated his son with a hug and soft words, Low gasped, "Does Zara know yet?" She gasped again. "Oh, my gawd, girl, you and Channa are pregnant at the same time."

Rommy bounced on her feet. "This is awesome."

Maya told Low, "My parents don't know yet. We'll tell them when we get home."

Low's lips thinned.

"Little bird," Dodge warned.

"What?" Low asked.

"You're keepin' a lid on it until Zara calls you."

Low rolled her eyes. "Of course I will."

"Shit," Dodge drew out.

Low waved a hand around. "Relax. I won't say anything. But please call me when you're telling them. I want to be on FaceTime or something."

Texas nodded. "You got it. We better hit the road, though."

Saint tossed his keys up and down. "I'll be driving you two."

They said another round of goodbyes and left with a final wave back to their family. Rommy hugged her mom.

"We'll see them soon enough," she said before shaking her by the arms. "You're gonna be a grandmother."

Low squealed and hugged Rommy again. "I think I want to be called Grammy."

Dodge walked over to them and kissed his wife's temple. "I like it."

"You should be, Pops," Rommy suggested before her eyes widened, "My food!" she cried and raced over to her plate.

Eve laughed and then called, "It can be warmed."

She put a protective arm around her dish. "Nope, I'm good."

Snorting, I asked Eve, "Want a coffee or some food?"

She faced me, her hands resting at my waist. "Can we go talk first?"

"Yeah." I nodded and took her hand to lead her upstairs to my room.

As soon as I had the door closed, she said, "I'm so sorry."

My throat tightened.

She wasn't second guessing this already, right?

Fuck me. I'm gonna shit myself.

"What for?" I slowly and gently asked.

Her brows shot up. "What for? For fucking this up. For being a bitch. For giving you mixed signals. For everything I said that was nasty. I never meant to be horrid, but I couldn't stop my mouth. I wanted to force every terrible thing I said to you back down my throat because... because I could see that it hurt you."

Her hands fisted at her sides as tears welled.

Moving over to her, I cupped the back of her neck, gripping her hair until she gave me her gaze. "We've been dancin' around each other for years, but I need you to know right now that you're worth the wait." Tears fell from her eyes, and her bottom lip trembled. "Sweetheart, I was more hurt for you when we had our moments because I knew you never meant any of it. You've been strugglin'. I saw it, felt it, but now that you've allowed me in, you don't have to handle this on your own. We'll deal with anythin' that comes up together, yeah?"

She gripped at my tee under my cut and dropped her forehead to my chest. "Damn you."

Chuckling, I asked, "Too much?"

She shook her head against me. "No. It was perfect. You always are. You made it easy to fall in love with you."

I stilled.

Did she realise what she'd said?

Licking my dry lips, I wondered if she could hear how wildly my heart beat.

Clearing my throat, I thickly said, "That's good. It means you're catchin' up to me."

That's good?

Why would I say that.

I sounded like a schmuck.

My damn ears rang from how fast my blood pumped through my body.

She tipped her head back. Red eyes and nose, tears brimming and falling, and yet she was still perfect. "I'm still going to freak out. I'll say the wrong things. I'll be a bitch when I'm uncomfortable from sweet and kind words or compliments. Are you sure you want me?"

Smirking, I leaned down and kissed her lips, her nose, and her cheek. "Sweetheart, I've been waitin' for you since the first time we slept together. Nothin' will stop me from wantin' you." When I saw the worry in her gaze, I added, "I know it ain't always gonna be smooth sailin' and there are things we've still gotta learn about each other, but all I need is for you to communicate with me. Let me know when somethin' is eatin' at your mind, and I'll do anythin' I can to help settle any worry you do have. I hope to do the same with you. Share what's on my mind too. It's gonna be trial and error, but we can rise above all the stuff that comes up and find what we're after in each other."

She blew out a heavy breath and pushed her face against my chest again. "I'll try my best, Quake. I really will because I've been in love with you for some time now. You deserve better, and—Hey!" she snapped when I pinched her ass.

"No negative talk about yourself. You're the best woman for me."

She groaned, dropped her face once again, and gently tugged at my tee where her hands were still fisted into the material.

"And I love you, too, Eve."

"Stop," she whined, making me chuckle. "But thank you."

"For lovin' you?"

She hummed.

"You're not hard to love, Eve."

She suddenly pulled back and looked up at me. "Promise me that if you get tired of me or you find someone else you're interested in, you'll tell me. I don't want us to end up hating each other if anything like that happens. Promise me you'll always be honest."

"I will," I said quickly. I already knew what that was about, how her parents cheated on each other and made it nasty at home about the affairs.

"And I promise too."

I nodded. "Can I ask somethin' of you then?"

"Anything."

"Call me by my name, not my club one."

She drew in a breath. "That means it's really real."

I smirked. "That's what we're goin' for, right? Somethin' real between us. Somethin' public. Somethin' where our love can grow."

"Oh my God," she breathed. "You need to quit being sweet. You're making me ache." Her face flushed. *Cute.*

"Baby, I'm gonna do a lot more to you soon too."

She leaned into me, head tipped back. "Okay, Kayson."

Fuck me.

My dick throbbed.

Never thought hearing my name from her lips like that would get such a reaction, but my body was lighting up with desire.

Groaning, I leaned down and claimed my woman's mouth.

CHAPTER THIRTEEN

EVE

A shiver ran down my spine. This was really happening. I told him I loved him. I did it.

I'd feared he wouldn't want me back, not like this, but his words had blown anything I pictured out of the water and eased my body into a frenzied state of need, want, and happiness.

Quake was mine.

No, *Kayson* was mine.

Every inch.

My heart hammered against my ribs, like it wanted to break free to be with his.

Could he feel how erratic it was?

Did he know he drove me wild with the way his tongue teased and twined with mine?

This felt different than all those quick romps in our bedrooms.

This was more.

It was the start of *us*.

Sliding my hands up his chest, I moaned into the kiss.

A need so strong to have him closer clawed at me.

We only pulled apart to catch our breath.

"Quake—Kayson," I quickly fixed, which made him smile and his eyes warm.

"Yeah, sweetheart?"

I scraped my top teeth over my bottom lip, my stomach fluttering when I was about to be so bold. "It's been a very long time."

"It has."

"And?"

He reached up to tuck some of my red hair behind my ear. "Did I tell you this colour is—"

I groaned. "We're not talking about my hair."

He smirked. "Then you need to eat breakfast."

"I had a protein shake earlier."

"Maybe I need to eat."

He hadn't had breakfast. He loved his food and was always in the kitchen, so I was surprised he hadn't had two platefuls already.

"Okay, we can—" I let out a gasp when he picked me up.

"I didn't say what I was gonna eat."

My pussy pulsed, and I bit my bottom lip, but a needy whimper escaped. I slid my hand to the back of his neck and pulled his head down to meet my lips in a hot and heavy kiss.

Kayson cupped my ass and ground into me, like he

wanted to show me how *I* made *him* feel. I dropped my head back and moaned as he trailed kisses down my neck.

"Jump," he ordered, voice low and rough.

I did, and he easily caught me before he took us to the bed.

Nipping at his neck, I told him, "You know I'm covered with birth control, and I haven't been with anyone."

"Me neither," he quickly added.

Smiling against his skin, I said, "I want nothing between us." We'd always used a condom so he'd know how important this was. "Kayson, I want you to come inside me bare. I want to feel your seed filling me."

He groaned. "Fuckin' hell, sweetheart."

Grinning, I pulled back and asked, "You like the idea of marking me deep?"

"Fuck yes," he clipped before sucking my bottom lip between his teeth and then biting down. Another moan rolled free since that bite felt like a claiming one. I rubbed myself against his hardness.

Kayson slowly released my legs, and I slid down over his strong body. As soon as I was on my feet, Kayson removed his cut and placed it on the window seat before he yanked his tee over his head, throwing it to the floor.

"God, I love your body," I told him, eyes roaming over his wide chest.

"Sweetheart, get naked. Need my mouth on you."

As he removed his boots and jeans, I made quick work of my clothes and climbed onto the mattress.

"Fuckin' hell," Kayson bit out as he watched me crawl up the bed, I glanced over my shoulder and saw him stroking himself. "Roll over," he ordered. "Show me what I want to eat."

Belly fluttering, I went to my back, then up on my elbows as I shifted my legs.

He groaned, swallowing thickly, stroking faster.

"Kayson" I whined, needing him.

"Sweetheart, you make my mouth water every fuckin' time." He stopped jerking to run his hand up and press it against his chest. "Make my heart act crazy. You're the best thing that's happened in my life."

"Kayson—"

"Nope. Won't fuckin' hear any different." He kneeled on the end of the bed. "You're mine now. I can say these nice things to you, and you can still get pissed or annoyed or shy about them but get used to me doing it more often and in front of people."

What could I say?

No?

I didn't want to. Not when I knew he'd been holding back for my sake.

God, I'd been such a bitch to him.

But no more.

Nodding, I smiled, "Okay, honey. Lay it all on me."

His grin was stunning and had my heart clenching.

He moved to hover over me and then leaned lower to kiss just above both nipples. My heart pounded as he leisurely licked, nipped, and sucked over each breast.

I wanted him inside me already. I needed to feel his cock for the first time without a barrier.

Still, he took his time lathering me with more kisses, licks, and then finally sucking my left nipple into his warm mouth. My pussy pulsed while I watched him pay attention to each side as I ran my hands up and down his arms.

But I couldn't take it anymore.

I had to have him.

"Kayson, *please*," I panted.

He hummed under his breath, enjoying my eagerness.

But he didn't move.

"Kayson."

I felt his smirk against my breast.

"I'm going to nut punch you if you don't move on."

He chuckled. "Don't you like my touch?"

"Yes, very much, but I really need your cock inside me."

He clicked his tongue. "I haven't finished yet." He kissed between my breasts and then trailed his wet tongue down over my stomach and then nipped at my trimmed mound, making me gasp.

He rested his chest on the mattress and then tucked his hands up under my ass. His heated gaze met mine, and he slowly leaned in for a long swipe of his tongue over my pussy.

"Fuck me, I love your taste."

I dropped down to the bed, panting, as he buried his face against me and made my body sing with only his tongue and mouth.

I ground down against his face, earning me a hum of approval.

"Kayson. Christ, yes. Oh God," I muttered, fingers digging into the sheets. Arching, I shivered. "Kayson," I cried out when he paid special attention to my clit. "God, please. Need you inside me. Please."

He gave me one last long lick and then climbed up my

body. I was never shy about tasting myself, which I knew Kayson liked, so when he kissed me, I poured all my want into it as I wrapped my legs around his waist, rocking up and down against his erection.

He pulled back to stare at me. His gaze was warmer than I'd ever seen before. "You're mine."

I nodded. "I am."

And I wouldn't take it back from him.

He rolled his hips against me, his cock brushing along my seam.

"Fuckin' love knowin' that you are. That I've got your heart."

I nodded. "It's yours."

"And you've got mine, sweetheart," he told me.

Lifting my hips against his, I teased, "Want something else of yours."

"Yours." He gripped his dick to guide it to my opening.

A grunted growl dropped from his lips when my walls tightened around him. God, he felt amazing sliding inside me uncovered. I tightened my legs around his waist and smiled up at him.

"Fuck me, Kayson."

His jaw clenched at my words, but he then asked, "You want me hard?"

"Yes. Need it. Want to come all over your big cock and have you fill me."

His jaw clenched again as he withdrew before thrusting back in hard. I gasped, nodding. "Yes, please." I hummed. "More of that."

He placed one hand to the bed as he fucked into me like a wild man while he held my stare.

"Yes," I panted. "Just there, babe."

"Sweetheart." As he pulled out, he glided his hand up to slide it around my neck. Feeling my erratic pulse, he thrust deep, his hand applying pressure.

Moaning, I pushed up into his touch, and his gaze darkened even more.

Something I liked a hell of a lot.

"Christ, Eve. You're fuckin' perfect." He fucked in and out, driving me crazy.

His hand left my throat to slide down and cup a breast. His gaze roamed over my body, like he didn't know where to keep his eyes.

I trailed my palms up his forearms and then to his back before raking my nails down. As soon as I did, Kayson threw his head back and groaned loudly, upping his thrusts.

When he suddenly pulled all the way out, I glared up at him.

Chuckling, he ordered, "Flip, want to see that amazing ass."

My glare vanished. Kayson watched while rubbing his hand over his wet cock as I got to my knees in front of him.

A gasp escaped me when he slapped my ass. I dropped to my elbows, jutting my butt back, but all he did was brush a hand over each globe.

"Kayson, please," I begged, wanting my man's cock back.

"Soon," he said.

I dug my fingers into the sheets when his fingers rubbed over my opening and down to my clit. He pinched, and I moaned.

I didn't fucking care if anyone heard me.

My man was bringing my body to life.

"Christ, sweetheart. Goddamn hot."

His tip brushed my entrance, and then, when he slammed into me, I cried out before moaning low as he pulled out and did it again.

He gripped my hips so he could fuck me over and over.

"Gonna fill your sweet pussy, Eve."

"Please," I panted.

"It's gonna be dribbling out of you, and I want to watch it."

I nodded against the mattress.

He threaded his hand into my hair and tugged my head back. "You like the idea of that?" he asked. "Of me fillin' you with so much, I'll get to watch it run out?"

"Yes," I whispered. His hand twisted in my hair more as he drilled into my drenched pussy.

He pulled all the way out again and ordered, "On your back."

I quickly rolled, and he pressed back in, fucking me while playing with my clit.

I was already on the edge, body tingling, but this drove me over.

"Kayson," I yelled, arching and coming, squeezing around his thrusting cock.

"Christ," he growled. "Here it comes, sweetheart." With the last few thrusts, he emptied inside me. He hummed and pulled all the way out, making me shiver.

Leaning back on his calves, he looked between my legs. His satisfied smirk made me grin as he watched his cum leak from me.

CHAPTER FOURTEEN

ROMANIA

"Die!" I snarled at the character on screen. Quake chuckled from his spot on the end of the couch as his character suddenly sliced my head off. "Dammit. How do you do it that fast?"

"Can't tell you."

"Can't tell you," I mimicked in a deep voice.

He chuckled again, and Eve, who was sitting between us, laughed too.

"You're such a sore loser," she teased, bumping into my shoulder.

Smiling, I nodded. "I really am. It's why Texas doesn't play with me anymore."

Quake snorted.

"I think it's time for a movie," Eve suggested. She leaned

into Quake, who put his arm around her shoulders, and they shared a sweet look.

Eh, they were sickly cute. It made me happy and annoyed seeing it. More happy than anything else. I was only annoyed because I didn't have that.

Standing, I told them, "I'm getting the popcorn. You two pick a movie."

"Grab some cookies too," Quake called.

"You got it, big guy." I skipped out and down the hall, greeting people as I went. It really was like home here. So many wonderful people were members. I wanted to get to know them all on the same level I did with the brothers in Caroline Springs.

My parents and I had been here for a few weeks now, and I already knew I'd miss this place and the people in it when I went home.

Especially Eve and Quake.

We'd been hanging out nearly every day. That was when I wasn't working on the bikes or Quake wasn't at the bar, and Eve wasn't working at her new job in a retail store. A place I wanted to visit because she had some kickarse clothes from there. Before she got this position, she used to work in a butcher shop that Death and Quake used to own before they sold them so Death could concentrate on his security business and Quake his bar.

In the common room, I waved to Blaze, Henri, Sawyer, and Arlo who were sitting with Lucas, West, and Adrick before I skipped into the kitchen and spotted Dusty.

"If I was a popcorn bag, where would I be?" I asked.

Laughing, she pointed to the pantry. "In there on the third shelf up the back. Near the chips."

"Thank you." I walked into the wonderland of so many goodies and called back, "And the cookies?"

"Did Quake make you ask?"

I poked my head out. "He did say to ask."

Dusty sighed. "He saw me making some. I knew it wouldn't be long for him to want some. They're on the cooling rack over there."

"Thanks again." I went back in the pantry, found the popcorn bag, and walked over to the microwave. While I waited for it to be cooked, I leaned against the counter and peeked in the large bowl Dusty had her hands stuffed in.

She snorted. "You and Quake with food. This will be meatloaf for dinner."

"Wicked, I love meatloaf. Mum makes it all the time, so I wonder if yours will be like hers or if it'll be different because we're in America. Do you need any help?"

"No, I'm good. Thanks, though, and hopefully you'll enjoy this as much as your mom's."

I opened the microwave and found a bowl to tip it into. "No doubt I will."

"Are you watching a movie with Eve and Quake?"

"Yeah." I smiled.

"You're close with Eve," Dusty commented.

I faced her. "Is that okay? Am I stepping on anyone's friendship toes? I can totally back off."

Dusty giggled. "Relax. I think it's good. Eve doesn't open up to many so it's wonderful to see how she is with you. And now she's.... I couldn't be any more thrilled than I already am at seeing her and Quake together. They were always made for each other."

I threw up a popcorn piece and caught it in my mouth. Around it, I said, "They really are."

"Rommy?"

"Dusty?" I grinned.

"Are you really okay with seeing them together?"

I jerked my head back. "Yeah, why?"

She shrugged, but then said, "It's none of my business."

I cocked my head to the side. "Dusty, I'd like to think we're friends—"

"We are," she said quickly.

I smiled. "Good. Then I want you to know that you can say anything to me."

She blew out a breath. "I just thought that maybe you have a small crush on Eve and Quake."

Groaning, I palmed my face. "Is it that obvious?"

She grinned. "I don't know if anyone else has noticed how you stare at them with heart eyes. No one has said anything to me." She shrugged.

"I hope not." Reaching out, I patted her arm. "And don't worry, I'd never do anything to jeopardise what they have. I'll be going home soon anyway, and it was never like something could happen."

Nothing would happen.

My smile faded, but I shook myself.

"I'd never think you'd try to come between them. You're a nice person, Rommy. The best since you're willing to bottle your own feelings to make sure they work on each other when they're new."

Shrugging, I gave her a thin-lipped smile.

I was also realistic. I lived in Australia, and they were in

America. I loved men and women, and they were loyal to each other.

Even though it would be a dream come true to have more with them both, it could never work.

"Hey, have you got a container I can put some cookies in?"

"Under the counter down the end there." She tipped her chin to the left. "And Rommy, whoever you end up with will be the luckiest person alive."

Laughing, I went to grab the container thinking how her words made me feel gooey on the inside. "Well, I hope they'll be alive. But thanks, Dusty. You're awesome, too, and you've got a smoking-hot old guy to brag about."

She blushed. "I did get lucky too."

"And you deserve it," I told her as I placed six cookies in the container and put on the lid. "I better get the food upstairs." I picked up the bowl of popcorn to balance it on the container. "One day soon, you and me are having a gaming day, deal?"

"Deal," she called before I walked out of the kitchen.

I'd only taken a few steps when Henri called, "Chéri, come here, please."

I detoured over to them at the table. "Hey, hi, hello." Smiles were given. "What can I do for you?"

"Where are your parents? I still haven't met them yet," Henri asked. "I would like our boys to meet them too."

I brightened and looked around. "They're here some-where. I can go find them and bring them here." I set the bowl and container down on the table.

"I would win," Adrick grumped, crossing his arms over his chest.

"Adrick, it's really not worth worrying about because it would never happen," West said.

"What's going on?" I asked because Adrick looked miffed over something.

Lucas rolled his eyes. "Wreck refuses to fight Adrick to see who would win."

"It would be me," Adrick said.

I eyed the man up and down and shrugged. "I don't know."

Adrick's dark gaze slowly turned to me.

"Adrick," West warned, taking hold of his arm.

There was a chuckle and then another Russian voice said, "I like this one."

Adrick snarled something in Russian, and then added in English, "So shut up, Dimitri."

I looked up at the man who'd just joined us. "Hi, I'm Rommy." I held out my hand. He looked at for a moment before taking it, and we shook.

"Dimitri. Adrick's second."

"Oh cool."

"Why do you not think I would win, little girl?" Adrick demanded.

West sighed.

Lucas groaned and dropped his forehead to the table.

Henri laughed. "He's like a dog with a bone." When Adrick shot Henri a glare, the French man squeaked and clung to Blaze's arm.

Blaze, who'd been just enjoying his coffee, shot a look at Adrick that had me wanting to pee myself. He was definitely thinking of bashing Adrick's head in.

Adrick waved him off. "Relax, I would not harm yours.

Even I know I would be breathing through a tube if we ever fought."

Blaze grunted and went back to drinking his coffee.

"But I would win against Wreck," Adrick added.

"Kid" was called, and I turned to see Mum and Dad walking our way. Dad had his arm around Mum's shoulders.

"Hey, come meet Henri, Blaze, Sawyer, and Arlo." I waved them over, but they were taking too long so I rushed to them, took their hands, and pulled them back to the table. "Henri, Blaze, Sawyer, and Arlo, these are my parents, Low and Dodge."

Blaze and Dad tipped their chins up, while Mum said, "Aren't you all just an adorable family."

"Thank you, chéri."

Mum's gaze widened. "That is a hot accent."

Henri cackled. "What is it people say? They call French the love language."

Sawyer rolled his eyes, but he was smiling too. Arlo just watched on with a big grin, until he said, "We're not living with them yet, but we will be. Sawyer and I aren't their real kids, but we wish we were. They're the best."

Nodding, I told him, "I bet they are." I thumbed to my parents. "They aren't my biological ones either. Dad's actually my uncle, and Mum was Dad's girlfriend when we came along. Well, she was when he wore her down." I winked, which had people laughing. "And since then, I've been the happiest in my life."

Arlo jerked up. "I am too. So happy."

"It's the best feeling, right?"

He nodded.

I glanced to Henri. Tears sparkled in his eyes. I mock whispered to Arlo, "I think Henri needs a hug from you."

Arlo jumped up and threw himself at Henri. It was lucky Blaze was there to help catch him.

"Little girl, why do you not think I would win?" Adrick said.

There was more groaning, and even Dimitri said, "You need to drop this."

"*Nyet.*" Adrick stared at me, waiting for an answer.

"You're both strong and big, but Wreck seems like the kind of guy that would break you in seconds."

"I am fast," he demanded.

I cocked a brow. "Then spar with me."

"What?" he asked with a smirk.

I bounced on my feet, loving this idea. "I wanna see how fast you are. Fight me and then I'll believe you could beat Wreck."

"Rommy, I don't think this is a good idea," Lucas said.

West nodded. "Adrick, don't even think about agreeing."

"She has asked for it," Adrick said, standing.

"Adrick," Dimitri started but shut up when Adrick raised his hand.

"Are we doing this?" Glee saturated my senses, and I skipped back to give us room while stretching my arms.

"Rommy's Daddy, you should stop this, oui?"

Dad shrugged. "She knows what she's doin'."

I loved the faith Dad had in me, but I also knew if Adrick did get the better of me, Dad would stop it.

"Kick arse, girl," Mum called.

Henri, Lucas, and West stared at them with wide eyes and gaping mouths.

I gave my parents the finger guns and a wink.

"Let's go, Adrick." I squatted down and stretched my left leg out and then the right.

Adrick cracked his knuckles, and his gaze seemed to dance with excitement too. He pretended he was casually strolling my way, but I knew as soon as he got close, he was going in for an attack.

Since I was still crouching and stretching my leg out, when he did go to strike, I quickly rolled out of the way and bounced up.

Grinning like a maniac, I asked, "Come on, you can do better than that."

Adrick smiled evilly at me. "You asked for it, little girl." He went into a fighting stance, but then quickly straightened and looked over my head. I wasn't falling for it. I heard that someone was approaching, but I wouldn't let whoever it was distract me.

"What the fuck?" Quake growled before his arm went around my waist and I was lifted off my feet.

"Wait, no. We were about to fight," I complained, tapping at his arm.

"That ain't happenin'," Quake snarled. He walked, with me held up against him, back to the stairs.

"I guess I win," Adrick called.

"No way. I'll be back," I snapped. "Come on, Quake, what the hell? You know I can fight."

He stomped up the stairs and, in my ear, he snarled, "I know. But he used to be with the Russian mafia. He'd play dirty just to prove himself."

Huh. Did he?

I didn't know that.

That meant Adrick would really go all out.

"Really?" I muttered, more to myself.

Quake stopped. "Fuck. Now you're really interested, aren't you?"

"Noooo," I drew out. "Not me."

He started moving forward again but still didn't drop me.

When we entered the room, Eve sat up from slouching on the couch. "What happened?"

Quake took us to the couch and dropped me onto it where I was half sprawled on Eve's lap.

"I found her downstairs ready to go head-to-head with Adrick."

"You were going to fight Adrick?" Eve yelled.

Groaning, I rolled over and kicked my feet over the couch armrest while leaving my head on Eve's lap. "I'd have won too."

Eve stared down at me, brows pinched as she brushed my hair back. "You also could have got your ass beat."

I grinned. "It'd be fun no matter."

Eve sighed. "What would your parents say about you fighting an ex-mafia man?"

Quake snorted, though he was still glaring down at me. "They were there watchin'."

Eve shook her head. "They're all crazy."

Laughing, I nodded. "That we are, but it's the best way to be. Hey, I forgot the snacks." I sat up. "I'll go and—"

"Nope," Eve said, pulling me back down. "You stay here. Kayson can go get them."

"Awww, that's—"

Eve covered my mouth as she blushed.

Quake bent and kissed her neck. "Be back. Tie her up if you have to."

I moved Eve's hand and yelled, "Kinky." But really, I didn't want to move. I liked that Quake and Eve were scared about me fighting Adrick, and I really was comfortable where I rested my head as Eve brushed her fingers through my hair.

"It's so long and thick."

I smirked. "Are we talking about my hair or Quake's dick?"

She snorted and then laughed. "You're an idiot."

I was.

An idiot for both of them.

Dammit, I was so screwed.

CHAPTER FIFTEEN

"*D*o you forgive me yet?" I asked Tech a week later, sliding into the seat beside him in the room we called church.

"Brother, if I hadn't seen my sister smilin' in the common room, it'd be a different story right now."

"Still, I am fuckin' sorry it was behind your back."

His jaw clenched. "Found out a while ago and was ready to cut you from my life, but someone had me seein' a different side. She didn't want to commit, right?"

I shook my head.

"Did she ask you to keep things quiet?"

I nodded.

"I get it. Though, no doubt I'll still want to punch you whenever I *think* about you keepin' this from me."

Snorting, I tipped my chin up. "I'll take it. It was a shit thing to do with the closest brother I have in the club."

"You dick. Don't say the right thing. Let me stay mad for a while longer."

Hell. Both of the Sager siblings couldn't handle nice words.

Rolling my eyes, I said, "I'll stop bein' understandin'."

He glared. "See that you do."

When Country entered, the door slammed closed, and he took his seat at the head of the table. "Torch, go get Dodge. He should be here for this." Torch slipped out of the room and was back moments later with Rommy's dad.

Country nodded towards a vacant chair that leaned against the wall. Not a seat at the table as those chairs were for patched-in members. When Dodge took it, Country said, "As of half an hour ago, the fuckers who trafficked all those people, the Murphy brothers, were assassinated."

Holy fuck.

That was the best news. As far as we knew, they'd dodged all attempts of obtaining them for questioning from the cops in Ireland.

Someone had found them and ended them.

"This is good, right?" Tech asked. "The ones who were kidnapped can breathe easy. No one else will come after them."

"Unless whoever snuffed them takes over the traffickin'," Wreck said.

Shit. There was that.

"Do we know anythin' more?" I asked.

There was a knock on the door before it opened and Blaze entered.

State cleared his throat and announced, "Blaze received a voice message from Malice, America's biggest kingpin in the mafia corporation, two hours ago." State placed an iPad on the table and hit Play.

"Blaze. Your little issue spilled over into my territory when the Murphy brothers caught wind of a certain hacker you know of because she, of fuckin' course, refused to leave things alone and got on their radar for it." Tech tensed beside me. "Since she's under my care while she works for me, I had to step in." He paused. "She's too valuable to lose. Months ago, the Sullivan family head in Ireland contacted me to see if I could help annihilate the Murphy brothers so they could take over. At the time I refused. Until now. I sent Reaper and his team to assist the Sullivans. By now you would have heard of their demise, and since I had my people help, I made sure I was promised a say in what businesses the Sullivans will continue with of the Murphys. Trafficking will no longer happen from Ireland. That business ended today. Tell your biker friends they can stop poking around. The Sullivans will follow my lead, and I swear that the Diamond MC and their family will be left alone. For this, I expect your respect when I say that you keep your contact with *my* hacker to friendship only. No business." The message ended.

I knew Blaze was connected to Malice. We'd had a meeting about it before Henri and Sawyer got taken. But I didn't know Tech knew the hacker. His reaction made me think he'd met her.

"Who's the hacker?" Gun asked.

"A friend," Blaze said.

"She safe working with Malice?" I asked.

Blaze grunted. "He won't let anything happen to her."

"This means no one will come after Rommy or any of the others now?" Dodge asked.

Country nodded. "Looks that way. We'll keep an eye on the Sullivans, but we can trust that Blaze knows Malice enough to accept what he said to be real."

Blaze nodded once. "They're safe."

We talked for a while longer, and when the meeting ended, I turned to Tech and asked, "You know this hacker?"

"When Blaze was on the phone to her, she slipped into our systems. Made me look like I was a baby who didn't know how to use my hands. Seems cool. I'm just a bit pissed I couldn't keep up with her and kick her out. I wasn't sure it was good she was workin' for Malice, but havin' him step in to make sure the Murphys don't get close to her says a lot."

I nodded. "He said she was valuable."

"With the skills she has, I can understand why."

Brothers started filing out of the room. "You and Blaze seem to have gotten close over the time of huntin' those ships."

He smirked. "You jealous?"

Rolling my eyes, I grinned. "Sure am. I miss my bro." I fluttered my lashes at him. "But seriously, was he the one who helped you see that it wouldn't be worth killin' me for being with Eve?"

"Yeah. He talked me down from murderin' you in your sleep."

"Then I'm damn grateful you two hang out doin' your computer stuff." Standing, I asked, "You comin' to eat lunch, or do you have to get back to Polished?" His computers were set up at Polished P & P, the escort club, since Henri started working there and Blaze wanted to be close to him.

"I'll grab some food before I head out." We walked out into the busy common room. I zeroed in on Eve, who was sitting beside Rommy. They were at a table with Rommy's parents.

Rommy leaned into Eve as she talked, and Eve watched her with humour in her soft gaze.

"They've really gotten close," Tech commented.

I stopped beside him as we watched them. "Yeah. She's helped Eve a lot."

Tech hummed. "Pretty sure Rommy was the one who got Eve to take the chance on somethin' public with you."

I grinned when Eve laughed at something Rommy said. "Without Rommy, I don't think Eve would have admitted anythin'. Eve had been scared and letting things hold her back, but then came Rommy encouragin' her. Gettin' Eve to open up and see the possibilities and then takin' that chance on us."

"Rommy's a pretty cool woman."

"Yeah," I said, but she was more than cool. There was something special about Rommy.

She was different, but in a way where she was easily accepted and stole a bit of your heart with how sweet and funny she was.

She was honest, curious, and most the time, no one could guess what was going to come out of her mouth. She cared too much sometimes, worried her differences would offend someone. Only it never would, not in our club. She was protective, and if something annoyed her, she sorted it right there and then. Like when Spider had snapped at her about the wheels on his ride, telling her she didn't know shit. She proved him wrong when she went on a tantrum about the right wheels for half an hour. He tried to walk off, but she just followed.

In the end, Spider sent back the wheels he'd ordered and got the ones Rommy had suggested. She was someone who anyone could connect with. She knew a lot and loved to share everything she did know.

I knew her and Eve connected on a different level to Eve's friendship with Dusty, and I could see how much Rommy cared for Eve.

I could also see the longing in her gaze when Rommy looked at Eve at times.

I only noticed since it was something I'd felt for a fucking long time.

Rommy was into Eve.

I should be jealous. They were close after all, but I couldn't be.

Not when Rommy had helped Eve in ways no one else had.

"Eve's never been this affectionate to the other women," Tech said as Eve leaned her head down to Rommy's shoulder, and Rommy rested her temple against it. They straightened when Low said something, and Rommy went on another word vomit, which was always cute.

"I'm not even sure if she's noticed how much they hang off each other. It's like that when we're doing anythin'. They gravitate to each other. A brush of their hand or hugging or leaning into each other."

"You okay with that?"

Why wouldn't I be? Eve was thriving.

But what happens when Rommy leaves?

Fuck. I wasn't sure how that was going to be, but we'd work it out.

"Have you seen your sister this happy?"

"Never."

"I can't be upset with their connection."

"I heard Rommy's bi. What would you do if they have somethin' more than friendship?"

"Then I'd share Eve because I'd give my woman anythin' she's ever wanted. Even if that means Rommy. All I want is for her to be happy and content like she usually is around me and Rommy."

Tech's gaze burned at the side of my face. He let out a whistle. "You've got it bad."

Grinning, I clasped him on the shoulder. "So damn bad."

"Wish you luck, brother."

"I'll wish you the same when you find yourself someone who'll put up with you."

He snorted. "Not anytime soon, thanks. Now, let's get some food."

I tipped my head to the table. "I'm gonna check if they've eaten."

He snorted and went towards the kitchen while I made my way over to the table.

When I placed my hand on each of their shoulders to show I was there, both of them tipped their heads up and smiled brightly at me. My throat closed over.

Christ, I couldn't deny that they were stunning.

"Hey, I'm grabbin' some food. You two need anythin'?"

Eve's smile turned soft. "I'm good, thanks."

"I'll take one of Dusty's raspberry and white-chocolate muffins," Rommy said, rubbing her belly.

Snorting, I tipped my chin up. "You got it."

It didn't take me long to grab a plate of food and Rommy's request, and I was soon back out at the table, sliding in on Eve's other side, just as Dodge said, "Kid."

Rommy had a mouthful, and bits sprayed when she said, "Yeah...? Oops," she added and picked a bit of chewed muffin off Eve's arm.

Eve stared down at her arm and then up at Rommy with her nose wrinkled up. "You're lucky I like you."

Rommy laughed. "I know." She faced her father again. "What's up, old man?"

"We're gonna start the plan to head home."

Rommy stilled.

Eve tensed.

Rommy put the muffin down, swallowed thickly, and asked, "Yeah? Um, when?"

"We've been here a month, so we're thinking at the end of next week."

We'd had only a month with them, yet it felt like a hell of a lot longer.

Low leaned forward. "Girl, no stress on us if you want to stay longer." Her gaze flicked to Eve and then me before swinging back to her daughter. "It's completely up to you."

Shit.

The thought of Rommy leaving put a foul taste in my mouth. It wasn't just because I knew Eve would miss her, but I'd grown used to having Rommy around, being the bright spark in everyone's lives in the club.

It'd be weird not hearing her voice or seeing her… seeing her smile or listening to her laugh or chatter.

Eve wasn't liking the idea either. She'd dropped her gaze to her lap, and she thinned her lips in a tight frown.

Reaching out, I took her hand under the table and squeezed it. When she looked up at me, I released her hand to curl an arm around her shoulders and kissed her temple.

I wanted her to know that I understood this would knock the wind out of her. Rommy had become such an important part in her life. A connection so strong that Rommy leaving would deeply upset her.

Hell, it upset me too.

Rommy picked at her muffin and then glanced at Eve and me. The look in her eyes had me thinking she was whimpering on the inside.

Like a wounded puppy.

But then she pushed it down, and for the first time, I watched as Rommy forced a smile as she said, "I can't stay away from work forever." She faced me and Eve. "One day you'll both have to come to Australia. There's so much I want to show you. Besides where I work, I can take you to the bar Pick and Billy own. The library that I love. Our home. I still live with Mum and Dad. I'd been saving to travel first, though. I've done enough of that for a while." She let out a little laugh. "At some point I'll buy myself a home where…." She shook her head. "Anyway, I could take you both to Ballarat where you'll meet Talon and see my brother's tattoo shop and go to Channa's bakery. I'd love for you two to meet everyone."

"You don't have to rush back, Rom," Dodge said.

Shaking her head, she shrugged and picked at the muffin. "We've probably outstayed our welcome anyway."

"So, you want us to grab you a ticket?" Low asked.

"Sure." She nodded.

She didn't sound sure at all.

Her parents shared a look as Rommy stood. "I'm gonna go grab a hot chocolate. Anyone want one?" When everyone declined, she rushed off to the kitchen.

Everyone looked at the muffin she'd left behind.

Yeah, this was hitting her hard.

I honestly didn't think she'd even considered going home.

"Our girl has a big heart. She'll miss you guys like I know you'll miss her," Low said.

Eve cleared her throat. "It won't be the same without her."

"Then you'll have to make sure to keep in contact," Low said. "At least there's video chat now. And besides, it is a great excuse for a holiday. Australia is an amazing place to visit."

"We'd like that," I said.

Eve smiled up at me, but it didn't reach her eyes.

How the fuck was this going to go?

Rommy leaving didn't sit well with me at all. My gut felt like lead.

I was determined to make sure we enjoyed the days we had left with Rommy here.

CHAPTER SIXTEEN

EVE

"Fuck, sweetheart," Kayson groaned into my ear as he pumped his hips back and forth. Moaning, I glided my hands up and down his back, then gripped his fine ass.

The wet slapping sounds were music to my ears.

He made me drenched each and every time.

My orgasm slammed into me, and I came hard, my fingers digging into his flesh. His lips landed on mine, and I whimpered into his kiss, still squeezing around his perfect cock.

His hips stuttered, and I drank his groan down as he finished inside me.

Smiling, I dropped my feet from being locked behind his calves to the bed. "So good," I murmured.

He kissed down my neck, nipping at my shoulder. "Christ, sweetheart. It gets better every damn time."

My smile grew as he rolled to his side next to me. I went with him, moving so I could face him. His cum leaked out between us. I didn't care if I got it everywhere, and neither did Kayson. We'd clean up later, but right now, we wanted to bask in the afterglow.

Reaching up, I brushed some of his damp, dark blond strands from his forehead. He took my hand and kissed the back of it.

"You've got a shift today, yeah?"

I nodded. "Rommy was coming with to check out the shopping mall."

"Tell her she can call me to pick her up if she gets bored."

God, he was the sweetest.

But he could be lethal when he needed to be. I'd seen him in many fights over the years.

With me, though, he was a big, warm teddy bear, and I loved it.

Scooting as close as I could, I pressed my face against his neck and kissed him there. "Love you."

His arm tightly wrapped around my waist, and his lips touched the top of my head. "Love you so fuckin' much, Eve."

It was ridiculous how melty this man made me.

I'd been a fool to fight this.

We were made for each other.

But it can still end.

He'll get bored. You're nothing. You're useless and pathetic and you'll just hurt him.

I burrowed in tighter and pushed those thoughts away.

I wouldn't destroy this.

Kayson wanted me.

He loves me.

And I refused to be the toxic part in this relationship that could fuck us up.

He made me happy, and he'd said I did the same for him.

Whenever he was close, it was like I'd been covered in a warm blanket, safe and protected, even from my thoughts.

I used to push him away in fear of being heartbroken, but no more.

I was going to hold on to the man I loved for the rest of our lives.

And I believed we would last.

I did.

But—

No!

We had the real deal. Nothing like those parents I had.

We were solid.

Tipping my head back, Kayson gave me what I wanted by kissing me. His slid his tongue into my mouth to dance with my own in a slow, dirty rhythm.

Unfortunately, there was a knock on the door.

Kayson groaned in annoyance before he yelled, "Wait." He climbed out of bed and slipped on some jeans. "I'll go get rid of them."

Grinning, I nodded and admired his gorgeous, big build as he walked towards the door. He opened it only a little so no one could see in.

"Dusty, what's up?"

"Get Eve in the shower. I'm taking her out for an early breakfast before she goes to work."

"I'll be ready in ten," I called, then laughed when I heard Kayson's deep sigh.

"Meet you downstairs," Dusty replied before Kayson shut the door, and I flung the blankets back, climbing out of bed. I quickly rushed into the bathroom and used the toilet before Kayson entered to turn on the shower.

He smirked. "If we have one together, it'll be longer than ten, so you go first. I'll play a game while I wait."

I kissed his jaw and stepped into the shower. "Thanks, honey."

He winked. "Welcome, sweetheart." His gaze ran down and up my body.

Laughing, I shoved his face back. "Tonight."

His grin made my heart stumble. "You should just move your things in here. Think about it," he said before closing the door to the shower and walking out of the bathroom like he hadn't just blown my mind.

He wanted me to move in with him.

Wasn't that too soon?

You've been dancing around each other for years.

But he didn't know everything. I'd never told him about the parents. And what happened if I did move all my things in and he grew bored of me?

Stop it, dickhead.

I promised myself I wouldn't think like that again.

It was going to be a hard process—to adjust the way I'd always thought—but it would be worth it. I'd continue this internal struggle until it eventually stopped. The outcome of staying strong with Kayson would be worth it.

After showering, I dressed in the clean clothes I brought in here for my sleepover.

But now he was asking for full-time sleepovers.

My stomach fluttered and heart stumbled.

Smiling, I removed the towel from my hair and went over to where he sat on the couch. He was blessed with one of the biggest rooms for his gaming set-up. It would be nice to have more space like this in our room.

Our room.

It wouldn't be just his, but ours.

Gripping the towel in front of me, I asked, "Are you asking me to move into your room?" I awkwardly laughed. "I did hear that, right?"

He put his controller down and stood, coming up to me. He took my towel from my hands and grinned. "That's exactly what you heard. But don't answer now. Take the day to make sure you could put up with me every night."

I scoffed. "It's more like if you can put up with me and my things lying around."

He cupped the back of my head and drew me in. "Always." He kissed me firmly before saying, "Have a good breakfast, sweetheart." Then he walked by me, with my towel, into the bathroom.

I blinked.

He wanted me in his space.

"Oh my God," I breathed, my smile amping up to a megawatt one.

"HE ASKED you to move into his room," Dusty exclaimed.

"Shhh," I said, looking around at the other customers in the café. Dusty waved me off, not caring who was around listening.

"I think this is amazing. You two have been dancing around each other for years." She reached across the table and took my hand. "Seriously, babe, I haven't seen you so happy in a long time."

I shrugged. Sitting back in the seat, I smiled. "Things are going well. I'm trying to not listen to the part of my brain that's a negative nelly, and I warned Kayson there'd be times when she wins."

"What did he say?"

"He's with me no matter what." I groaned in annoyance at how smitten I sounded. "That man has turned me into a marshmallow."

Dusty laughed. She pushed her empty plate to the side. "I don't think it's just from Quake," she said softly.

"What do you mean?"

"Eve" was all she said, brows high, her tone pointed.

I knew what she meant.

Rommy.

She'd touched my heart in ways I never expected.

I loved having her around. I loved seeing her and Kayson interact. I loved her laugh and everything she said because I never knew what was going to come out of her mouth next.

She's so sweet and funny and also strong and fierce.

She was under my skin in a way I'd never felt before with any other woman.

Rommy was special.

She made me warm and relaxed. So much so, it was easy to switch off my brain when she was around. A lot like I managed when I was with Kayson.

"You're talking about Rommy."

Dusty nodded. "Yeah."

Sighing, I rubbed a hand over my face and tucked some of my hair behind my ear while I thought of a way to explain myself, but I was coming up blank.

"Do you notice Rommy's very affectionate?"

Snorting, I nodded. "Of course. It's not hard to miss." She was always touching and leaning or hugging against Kayson and me.

"Okay, so you don't mind she's like that with Quake?"

I jerked my head back, eyes widening as my pulse raced. It had never crossed my mind.

Why hadn't it?

If it were anyone else—if one of the club girls rubbed themselves up against Kayson or hugged or brushed their hand over him—I'd see red. I'd tell them to back off, and yet, with Rommy it was... normal?

Dusty laughed lightly. "What's going through your mind?"

I sat back but then leaned forward. "Why haven't I been jealous?" Why did I like sharing my time with the both of them together?

Why did the thought of Rommy going home feel like my

chest caved in and the only person keeping me whole was Kayson?

Would he miss her?

"Dusty...."

"You two have bonded in a way that's different to your friendship with me and the other women. I love that you have something special with Rommy. She's an amazing woman. But maybe think about the type of connection it is. Could it be more than friendship?"

I scoffed, snorted, then laughed. "What? No. *No.* I've never.... I wouldn't cheat on Kayson. Ever."

She shook her head. "That's not what I'm saying. I know you'd never leave Quake. You two are committed completely. But there's nothing wrong with adding a third."

"What?" I breathed.

A third?

Huh?

"No. I... no. That's like cheating."

"It's not. Did Rommy ever tell you about her friend Josie who's married to two bikers, Pick and Billy? It does happen, and there's nothing wrong with that."

"I'm not into women," I told her.

I wasn't. Never had it crossed my mind either.

And yet the image of Rommy smiling at me as she leaned in—

Whoa. What the fuck?

"Sorry if this is freaking you out," Dusty said softly. "I just wanted to bring it up before Rommy leaves. I'd never want you to regret anything. I always feared that with you and Quake. Though, that's sorted now." She gave me a tight-lipped smile. "Sorry. I shouldn't have said anything."

She shouldn't have.

I never would have considered that three people in a relationship could be happy. That was absurd. Crazy.

"Don't worry about it," I told her. "It's not like that for us. Kayson and I are just close friends with Rommy."

Dusty nodded. "Okay, yeah. Now, do you have time for another coffee, or do you need to get back for work?"

I pulled out my phone and saw the time. "I should get back." Standing, I asked, "Another time?"

"Always." Dusty smiled. "And you know I'm here for you, Eve. For anything."

"I know. You know I appreciate you and the other old ladies."

She bumped into my hip as we walked out. "We know."

When we got back to the compound, I quickly went to my room and dressed in a classy, knee-length dress and heels. The store I worked in was more upper-class fashion, so I had to make sure I looked decent. I applied a small amount of make-up and headed downstairs to see if Rommy was in the common room.

I found her there sitting with a very pregnant Raya and Raya's sister, Wrenley.

Swallowing thickly, I ignored the extra beat to my heart and made my way over.

Rommy waved her hands around while she talked. Until she settled down so she could rub Raya's stomach. The woman was going to pop out her and Death's baby any day now.

"Hey," I called.

"Eve!" Rommy exclaimed, jumping up from the couch and running over to wrap me up in a hug.

My ears rang from how hard the blood rushed through me.

She tipped her head back and beamed up at me. "How was breakfast?"

"Kayson tell you?"

"Yep. Then I beat him at a couple of games before I came down here." She moved back, and we walked over to the couch.

"How have you been, Eve?" Wrenley asked.

"Good." I smiled.

"Aww, look at that smile. She's so in love with Quake," Rommy teased.

I wrapped an arm around her to cover her mouth. "We're going. You two take care. And I know I've said it a million times, but I want to know as soon as you're in labour, Raya."

"Wrenley has a list on who to text. The waiting room will be full."

"Just like when Dusty had Seth."

Raya nodded. "But hopefully Leland won't nearly pass out like Country did."

Grinning, I held up my crossed fingers. "Later, ladies."

"Bye," Wrenley said.

"Have fun," Raya called.

Hand in hand, Rommy and I started walking towards the door, like it was the most natural action in the world. Like we'd done it a billion times instead of the few we had. Only this time, my heart stumbled. "Are you sure you won't get bored?"

"Quake said if I do, he'll pick me up. But I doubt it. I haven't shopped the trillion times Mum has."

See, knowing Kayson would pick Rommy up and they'd be alone and Rommy would probably touch him in some way didn't bother me.

Did that make me a bad person for not being jealous?

I glanced down at Rommy as she rambled on about the food she wanted to try at the shopping mall.

It was so easy to hold her hand as we walked. We'd done it many times over the weeks.

She's really pretty.

Gorgeous long, dark hair, stunning dark blue eyes with what looks like a black ring around the outer edge. A cute, pert nose, and a body that was sexy and strong.

Yes, I was on the shorter side, but nothing like Rommy.

It always surprised me at how someone so tiny was as lethal as she was.

Was I attracted to Rommy?

Could I picture kissing or touching her?

My body warmed as my belly fluttered.

What did that mean?

And what did Kayson think of Rommy? I knew they got along, but was he attracted to her?

Blowing out a breath, I shook my head as I told myself that figuring it out wasn't magically going to happen in seconds. I might not even have all the answers before she left for Australia.

We were oceans apart. She loved her home, and I loved mine.

I couldn't ask her to stay and put her life on hold just so we could spend more time together so we could work out where this was going.

What I did know was that Rommy was our friend, and

we needed to enjoy the time she still had with us without putting more pressure on ourselves.

Besides, I doubted Rommy was into Kayson and me.

She was just a loving and affectionate person.

With everyone.

Right?

CHAPTER SEVENTEEN

ROMANIA

There was so much to look at in the shopping mall. I'd already found gifts for some of the brothers in the club back home and dropped them off to Eve so she could look after them. It was highly likely I was going to have to post this stuff home because I doubted everything would fit in the suitcase my parents brought from home for me.

Now I was looking for something for Eve and Quake. But I wasn't sure what.

What did I know about them?

Eve enjoyed energy drinks and protein smoothies, reading non-fiction—*ick*—watching action movies, and Quake.

She already had him, which I believed I helped with, but she needed something else. Something to remember me by.

Then there was Quake. He loved food, gaming, working in his bar, and Eve.

I needed to find something that whenever they looked at it, they'd think of me.

Wait, wait, wait.

Taking out my phone, I opened the photos. The other day we'd been sitting on the couch when I snapped a picture of the three of us. Eve and Quake were cuddled up behind me and I was giving the peace sign while smiling like a lunatic.

It was perfect.

I just needed a place to print it out and find a frame.

With a plan in mind, I set off to figure it out. Thankfully, when I asked some people, they were happy to point me in the right direction.

By the time I had my gift done, it was an hour later, and I totally deserved an iced chocolate. And maybe Eve would like a coffee too.

With the bag on my arm and two drinks, one in each hand, I made my way back to the clothes store where Eve worked.

I'd just entered, when Eve's manager Anna raced up, asking, "Did you see security?"

"No, what?"

"Back left corner two people are hassling Eve and won't leave."

My gut dropped, and I raced towards the area she said. When I rounded the corner, I heard, "Think you're fancy now? That your shit don't stink? You're still nothing."

"Hey!" I called, stalking over.

The woman turned while the man whispered something to Eve that had her paling.

"What the fuck you want, bitch?" the woman snapped.

I threw the iced chocolate in her face, plastic cup and all. When she screamed in outrage, the guy turned and charged. I had one hand free, but maybe I wouldn't even need it. The old guy was obviously intoxicated with the way he was stumbling.

When he got close, I crouched and swept my leg under his feet. He stumbled and dropped. Before he could get up, I pressed my boot down on his throat.

Holding the coffee cup over his head, I demanded, "Don't move unless you want to be burned."

When he went to say something, I pressed on his throat harder. He quit squirming and snapped his lips closed.

I looked at Eve, who seemed like she wanted to lose her breakfast as she leaned against the wall. If it hadn't been here for her, I was sure she'd be on her bum.

"Eve?" I called.

Her gaze swung to me, tears welling.

"What do you want me to do?" I asked.

The woman gripped at me. At my hair and tee, she pushed and pulled. Pinched and slapped, yelling, "Get off him, you whore. Leave him alone."

"Eve?"

"Security. Step away from each other." The guard held up a Taser and waited for me to release my foot. When I moved off to the side, I placed the coffee cup on one of the shelves and watched the old guy sucking in some hard breaths before the woman dropped to her knees next to him.

"It's her fault. She attacked us," the woman screamed. "Darling, are you okay?"

The guy shoved her back and sat up. "I want to press charges," he said.

"No!" Eve exclaimed. She straightened and took a step closer. "She was saving me. They came in here and started shouting and threatening. Anna witnessed it." Eve pointed to her nodding manager.

"They noticed Eve up front. She tried to walk off quickly, but they followed her. They shoved her and got in her face. She did nothing to provoke them, and then Eve's friend arrived to try and help Eve by moving them away."

"She threw a drink in my face," the woman bellowed.

"Lewis, going to need a hand in Rosies," the guard said into his walkie-talkie.

"*On my way*," Lewis replied.

Slowly, I shifted over to where Eve stood shaking. Reaching out, I took her hand in both of mine to hold them against my chest. "Are you okay?"

She shook her head.

Gently, I pulled her into a hug. "Do you know them?" I whispered.

I turned when I heard the guard instruct, "On your feet and come with us."

"But it wasn't us. It was them," the woman barked. The guards didn't listen to them, and they got the couple to their feet before they escorted them out.

The woman didn't shut up, though. "You stupid bitch. You're doing this to your own parents. You ungrateful little slut."

Her parents?

Her fucking parents acted like this and said those horrid things to her.

I wanted to hurt them again, but worse than I already had.

If I'd known who they were, I would have done more.

Facing Eve, I took her hand and led her to the back room before shutting the door on the woman's screaming.

"Fuck," Eve muttered, hands covering her face.

I took her wrist, guiding her over to a seat. When she sat, I crouched in front of her, placing the bag with her and Quake's gift on the floor beside me. "Don't listen to a thing they said, Eve." I rested a hand to her knee. "There are people in our lives who don't deserve to be there. Those people are two of them. What they say means nothing. They don't know you, and they'll never have the chance to know how amazing you are. Fuck them."

She drew in a shuddering breath. "Fuck them."

I smiled. "Exactly. Now, I'm going to suggest you take the rest of the day off. We can grab some takeaway, go back to the compound, and relax while watching one of those movies you like to rewatch. Or we could get drunk. Or I could leave you with Quake so he can snuggle all the love into you, like you deserve, so you know you're wanted and needed and important. Because you are, Eve. You're fucking awesome."

She dropped forward to rest her forehead on my shoulder. My heart hammered. I hoped I didn't overstep or suggest the wrong thing. I didn't want to upset her. She was already hurt by those horrid cock-sucking pricks.

Should I text Quake to tell him what happened?

Maybe I should let Tech know about it, too, since those

people were connected to him as well. He'd likely want to make sure they never talked to Eve again.

Hell, Quake and Tech would probably want to pay those fuckers a visit, and I'd love to go with them too.

The door opened, and Eve slowly straightened up. There were no tears, thankfully.

Standing, I turned to Anna and gave her a tight smile.

"Anna, I'm so very sorry this happened," Eve said.

"Eve, don't worry, please. I just wanted to check if you're okay."

She stood, straightening out her dress. "Yes. I'm fine."

"I have Kate coming in. I want you to take the day, honey." She walked forward and squeezed Eve's shoulder. "Go home and brush this event away."

Eve nodded. "Thank you, Anna."

"You're a great manager, Anna," I told her.

She waved me off. "It's what anyone would do when an employee is being hassled."

"Somehow, I'll make sure they never come back to the store," Eve said.

Anna gave her a sympathetic smile. "Even if they do, someone else will handle it. You shouldn't have to, Eve. Then we'll call security right away."

Eve drew in a shuddering breath as tears filled her eyes. "Thank you." Anna squeezed Eve's arm before heading back out front.

Eve turned to me. "I'll just grab my bag." I nodded, and while she dipped away, I quickly shot a text to Quake.

ROMMY:

Eve had a situation at work with her so-called parents. Tell Tech and maybe both of you be there when I get her back to the compound.

His reply was nearly instant.

QUAKE:

I'll come pick you both up.

ROMMY:

No. I'll drive Eve home.

QUAKE:

We'll be waiting.

Pocketing my phone, I picked up the bag and glanced at the inner door just as Eve walked through.

I smiled. "Ready? I'm going to drive us back."

She frowned. "I can do it."

"I know you can, but let me have a go at driving in America. I promise not to drive on the other side of the road. The *correct* side."

She snorted, but her amusement quickly vanished, and she quietly said, "Okay."

Hand in hand, I led us out to the car, got her into the passenger side, and then I slid into the driver's seat.

"Feels weird on this side." I started the car and backed out. "Fang bought an American car. I haven't been in it, but I've seen it. The motor on that baby sounds like a purring cat." I rambled on about the car and then went on some more about other types of vehicles the brothers had. "But me, I love a VW Beetle. You know, like on the old movie *Herbie*. I also adored *Transformers* too. Now those movies were brilliant…. Here we are."

Eve had been watching me talk, and when she looked out the front windscreen, her eyes widened.

"Did I distract you enough?" I asked, stopping at the gates until they opened.

"You did. Thank you, Rommy."

"I've got your back," I told her.

When we drove in, I parked near the front door just as it opened.

Quake and Tech strode over to the car. I heard Eve's breath catch as her door was pulled open, and Quake helped her out, hugging her close when her first sob broke.

My chest ached.

I knew she'd been holding it in at work.

But I also figured she'd want to be warmed by Quake's arms when she let her feelings crash.

When I stood by the front of the car, Tech approached with a strained look on his face. Like any sibling, we didn't like seeing our sisters or brothers upset.

"What happened?" he asked.

"When I got there, they had Eve cornered and were saying crappy stuff to her."

"Fuck," he clipped. "I let this happen. I should have done—"

"Nothing," Eve said. She sniffed and wiped at her face. "Back then we didn't have the club. It was you and me against them when we were young. We did what we could."

Tech ground his teeth together. "They have no fuckin' right to even approach you."

"It was a shock, and the stuff they said was shit. It'll probably mess with me a little, but I refuse to allow it to stick anymore. I'm worth something."

"Fuck yes," I yelled, pumping the air with my fist.

Eve and Quake gave me a warm smile.

"Still, I'm gonna make sure they don't visit you again," Tech said with a wicked grin, like he was already picturing what he was going to do or say.

"I think Rommy probably scared them away."

Tech grinned. "What did you do?"

I shrugged. "Nothing much. I wish I could have done more."

"Rommy, what did you do?" Quake asked.

"Threw a drink in the woman's face and kicked out the guy's legs so he fell down."

"Then pushed her boot onto his neck so he couldn't get back up while threatening to throw a hot coffee on his face," Eve added.

The men chuckled.

"Damn, I wish I'd seen it," Tech said.

"Rommy, come here," Eve said.

I quickly skipped over, and she brought me into a tight hug. "Thank you."

Quake's arms swept around both of us, and he pressed his lips to my head. "You're pretty cool, Rommy."

I grinned up at him and then looked to Eve.

God, I wanted to kiss them both.

The longing to be with them both made my heart clench.

Instead of trying my luck and ruining everything, I rolled my eyes and moved out of their embrace. "It's what friends do." I needed a distraction. Stat. Thankfully, I remembered I had the best type of one. "Wait," I called as I rushed back to the car. "I almost forgot." I grabbed the bag and brought it over to them, holding it out to Eve. "Before I leave for Australia, I wanted to get you both something. It's just something small." I quickly turned to Tech. "Sorry I didn't get you anything." He smirked and waved me off. "But, uh, yeah, this is like a thanks for putting up with me while I've been here and don't forget about our friendship while I'm not here."

I wish you both cared about me like I do you.

My feelings had grown so big, they were taller than me.

They were the best people I knew, and I knew a lot of great folks.

Quake and Eve were just different than anyone else.

How fucked up was it that I'd found my people who I could fall for, yet they'd never see me in that way?

And I'd never come between them.

Besides, I couldn't pick. I'd be greedy and want both.

Eve opened the box the frame came in, which was blank, so it didn't give anything away until she pulled it out and saw the image of the three of us.

"I know it's goofy, but I really like that picture of all of us."

Eve's watery gaze met mine, and she hugged it to her chest. "It's perfect."

I scoffed, waving her off while my heart spasmed at her sweetness. "It's nothing really."

"It's a great gift, Rom," Quake said.

Eve nodded. "It'll go on the television stand in our room."

I saw Quake's body jolt before he swung his gaze down on Eve. "Our room?"

Eve faced him, tipping her head back. "Yeah. If the offer to move into your room is still available."

"Fuck, sweetheart, yes. A million times yes." He looked at us and back down to Eve.

"Go, sweep her off her feet and take her to the room, you caveman," I teased, trying my hardest to ignore another pang to the chest.

Quake grinned and did just that. He picked her up and walked her inside while I watched them go.

"So," Tech drew out, "how long you been into my sister and Quake?"

CHAPTER EIGHTEEN

ROMANIA

$\mathcal{I}$ snorted and coughed. "What? Ha, no. Where are you pulling that from?" I scoffed and started for the door myself. "You're crazy." How had he seen this? Was I that obvious? Oh shit, did they know? Did anyone else? I had to hide it better.

"Want to come with me to see those birth pricks?" he asked. Aww, he was being sweet and changing the subject.

He probably saw my pure panic and wanted to ease my emotions.

Still, I had to be sure this subject would be dropped before I either shit myself or vomited from worry that I'd been too obvious with Eve and Quake. I never wanted to ruin anything for them.

Spinning around, I raised a brow and asked, "Are you going to talk to me about feelings?"

He smirked. "Not if you don't want me to."

I grinned. "Then I'm totally on board to teach those people a lesson."

Saint and my dad suddenly walked around the corner. "Whose arse are you beatin'?" Dad asked.

"The people who brought Eve and Tech into the world," I offered.

He stopped and crossed his arms over his chest before looking to Tech. "Need a hand?"

Saint clapped and then rubbed his hands together. "I'm always up to scarin' some people."

Tech nodded. "Appreciate the hand. Let's make sure they get the picture, they're not to show their fuckin' faces to either of us again." He took Eve's keys from me, and we climbed into the car.

Saint and I were sitting in the back when he asked, "So why doesn't Rommy want to talk about feelin's?"

I slapped at his arm. "Nothing. Shut up."

"This about you likin' two people?" Dad asked.

Groaning, I palmed my face. "Does everyone know?"

"Yep," Tech said.

"Sure do," Saint replied.

"Easy to read," Dad said.

"Do *they* know?"

God, I hoped they didn't.

"Don't think so," Tech told him.

"How the hell did you read this with Rommy, but you didn't know about Quake and Eve for years?" Saint asked him.

He paused to think about it, then said, "Fucked if I

know. Maybe, subconsciously, I never thought a brother would do that to me."

"You still cut about it?" Saint asked.

"Already told Quake I forgive him, but I get to punch him any time it comes to mind and pisses me off again."

The guy's chuckled, but I was just glad we were off the subject—

"Back to Rommy," Saint said.

"Dick," I muttered, then louder, I said, "No, we are not back to Rommy. We're off this subject all together. I live in Australia, and I'd never jeopardise what Eve and Quake have. They're just starting out, and it's a forever type of relationship. I wouldn't mess that up for them. Now, Tech, I'm guessing you know where these people will be. They couldn't still be caught up with security at the mall, right?"

"Shit, I didn't think of that. Dodge, plug my phone into Eve's car there." After Dad did that, Tech hit some buttons, and Blaze's name lit up.

"Yeah?" Blaze answered.

"Hey, need a favour. Look up Michelle and Jim Sager. Check their address, but I also need you to hack their phones to see their whereabouts."

"You need help?"

"Thanks, but I've got a group in the car with me."

Blaze grunted. "Good."

"Hi, Blaze," I called.

There was silence for a moment and then he commented, "Nice pick on takin' the hellcat."

"Awww, you have a pet name for me. Can I make one up for you?"

"No," he replied blandly before he ended the call.

Grinning, I rolled my eyes. I liked teasing that man. He was easy to rile.

"We're just gonna head to the last I have for them until Blaze can confirm it," Tech informed us.

Dad looked at Tech. "How long does—" The phone rang with Blaze's name lighting up.

Tech grinned at Dad before he answered. "Blaze."

"Phones are saying they're both at home." He gave us the address, and Tech nodded.

"Thanks, man," Tech said.

Blaze grunted and hung up.

Dad snorted. "Is he always like that?"

Tech and Saint chuckled, but it was Tech who said, "Yeah, but you learn not to take it to heart. He's a good guy. Just rough around the edges."

"Except with Henri," I said.

Tech nodded. "Except with Henri, Sawyer, and Arlo. But if anyone fucks with them..." Tech shook his head. "They'll be dead."

"He used to deal in body parts," I told Dad.

He swung his wide gaze around to me. "For real?"

"Yep." I bobbed my head. "Henri told me about it the other day. It was what broke them up ages ago, but then Henri called Blaze to help rescue Dusty and they reconnected. Blaze gave up that business so he could keep Henri. He won't let anything come between them again."

Dad huffed. "Takes a good woman or man to come along and wake you the fuck up."

"Damn right. Kylo was that for me. One blow job later I was a goner," Saint said.

Tech groaned, Dad chuckled, and I grinned before I asked, "Seriously? One BJ and you were obsessed?"

"Please don't ask him," Tech complained.

"Fuck yes I knew he was meant to be mine."

I nodded. "That's pretty cool. Maybe I need to get Gun to teach—"

"Fuck's sake, kid," Dad yelled.

Tech snorted before he laughed while Saint just roared his mirth.

Smiling, I shrugged. "Just saying I'd like to find my own one day."

"Or two," Saint commented.

I shoved him. "Zip it, peen head."

"Dodge, you and Low are gonna be missed, but it really won't be the same without our girl around," Saint said, making me all buttery.

"Aww, you like me." Stretching over, I hugged him, which he returned before patting my head awkwardly.

Dad turned, smiling softly. "She has that way about her where everyone likes her."

"Not everyone," I reminded him.

He scowled. "Fuckin' teens."

"What happened?" Tech asked.

"There was a group of girls who absolutely hated me because I talked too much. They were popular and had these guys hassle me. Used to stick things in my locker, corner me in the hallways, push me, punch me, spit in my face." Dad's hands fisted at the memory. "Relax, Dad, you guys took care of it."

"Only after you'd been dealin' with it for years. She'd go to school like nothin' bad was happenin' and put up with everythin' because she thought that one day they'd get over whatever they hated her about and become friends."

"Yeah, yeah. I learned that not everyone is nice. It hurt my heart to know that they could hate someone because they're different. So, when Dad, Mum, and Texas found out, the first thing Dad had to do was lock Mum down since she was so mad she would have actually smacked some kids around and got into trouble for it. Then Dad, Texas, and some of the other brothers rode to the high school."

"Did you kick their asses?" Saint asked.

I giggled. "I'd already heard my family arrive, so when the last bell rang, and I knew they'd come to hassle me again, I raced outside. They followed, of course. You should have seen their faces when they saw me surrounded by my family. *Best day ever.* Dad stalked up to the group and threatened that if they didn't leave me alone, they'd deal with the brotherhood."

"They left you alone after that?"

"Yep. They sure did, and that was when I started to learn how to fight so any other problem I had, or someone else who was different had, I could step in to help."

"How in the hell have you stayed so positive when you've dealt with the shit you have in life?"

"Because I've been surrounded by people who love me and have shown me it's okay to be who I want to be. I don't need to be defined by a prognosis. I'm just here living life and enjoying every moment I can while helping protect those who have trouble standing up for themselves."

"Christ, Rommy," Tech said. "You're like a ray of damn sunshine, and I mean that in the best way possible. You've warmed so many damn lives, my sister for one. She's been brighter since you've come into her life, and I can't thank you enough for it."

I waved him off. "That's sweet. Thank you. But I don't think I've done anything special. I just wanted to be her friend and help her see that her man is scrum-diddily-umptious."

Saint snorted. "You're a good egg, Rommy. Though, your taste in guys needs to be checked."

"Hmm, if I wasn't attracted to Quake, then I'd say the next guy I found hot would have been Gun."

Saint glared. "Back the fuck off, bitch."

Laughing, I rolled my eyes. Even Dad and Tech were grinning wide.

"And now I'm pumped to hurt someone," Saint commented.

I stuck my tongue out at him, which made his lips twitch.

"That's good then, since we're here." Tech pulled the car to a stop outside a rundown weatherboard home with long lawn and weeds. Even the porch looked like it could fall at any moment.

"Was this where you and Eve lived?" Saint asked.

Tech hummed under his breath, taking in the house. His jaw clenched before he unlocked it to say, "Let's get this shit done." We all climbed out and made our way to the front door.

When Saint stepped onto the porch behind Tech, it groaned, and Dad quickly pulled Saint back just as a piece of wood collapsed.

Tech didn't knock. He lifted his foot and kicked it in with a loud crack.

"The fuck?" Jim yelled.

Tech entered, and we quickly followed, jumping the porch to get inside.

"Remember me?" Tech demanded, crossing his arms over his chest.

"That bitch ran to complain to her brother. Get the fuck out. Don't want anything from you."

"You!" Michelle screeched as she strode down the hallway, eyes locked on me.

"Kid," Dad said.

I moved around the men and rushed the advancing woman. I ducked, and since I was moving fast, I was able to pick her up and slam her down to the grotty carpet. I straddled her waist and held her wrists to the floor with one hand.

"Get off me," she screamed.

I slapped her. "Shut up."

"You bitch."

I slapped her again. "Quiet," I warned.

"Get that stupid bitch off her," Jim snarled. He advanced my way before Tech lunged and punched him in the face. Jim staggered back, eyes wide.

Tech grinned a pretty smile. "Been wantin' to do that for a fuckin' long time."

Jim's gaze narrowed. "You have no right—"

"No right?" Tech clipped. "You and that cunt beat, starved, and would have pimped us out so you could stay high or drunk."

Hearing the words, I slapped Michelle again.

"I didn't move," she snapped.

"No, but I hate hearing the shit you did to your own

kids. You're supposed to love them, take care of them." Hell, fury burned under my skin. I slapped her again.

"Enough," Jim yelled. "Just leave us alone."

"Then make sure you never step foot in that mall again. Make sure you and that bitch stay far away from me and Eve for the rest of our lives. If you don't, I'll come back and kill you. We have a good family at our backs now so know it won't just be us you'll have to deal with. And you really won't like it if we see you again in any fuckin' way." He stepped in and jammed his fist into Jim's stomach. The guy dropped to the floor, hands up and out.

He groaned. "Okay, okay, you won't see us again."

"Rommy," Dad called.

I grinned down at Michelle and leaned down to whisper, "I'd have done more damage so think yourself lucky." With a final crack of my hand to her face, I bounced up and over to the others.

Dad nodded once, while Saint grinned and cupped the back of my neck, shaking me slightly.

I hadn't been lying either. I really did want to beat on her some more for spewing those vile things to Eve and making her think she wasn't worthy of love.

In a way, I hoped they didn't listen, and I'd get to pay them a visit again.

Then I remembered I wouldn't be around for much longer, and my stomach twisted.

CHAPTER NINETEEN

QUAKE

A smile tugged my lips up as I watched Rommy touch up Eve's red hair with the dye. She was rambling on about the time she was on a school trip to the Ballarat Wildlife Park when all the kangaroos were in heat or something because there was a lot of action happening around them.

I was going to miss her so fucking much.

In two days, she'd be gone.

Eve laughed at something, but I was only half listening while I watched them together. They gravitated towards each other all the time. Hell, I was even under their spell to be close and touch in some way.

Like now, I was on my side lying along the couch with Rommy sitting in the crook of my waist, and Eve was on the floor between Rommy's legs with her arms slung over each of Rommy's knees.

She was one of us.

Rommy belonged at the Diamond MC. Hell, even Tech and Saint would agree. Their praise for her the other day when they'd come back from dealing with those fuckers was high. They adored her. Thought of her as a sister.

She should stay.

But we couldn't ask her to give up her family just for us.

Christ, they looked gorgeous together.

I could imagine Eve tipping her head back and Rommy leaning down to kiss—

Abort that fucking thought immediately.

Rommy was close enough to my junk she'd feel my dick grow.

But hell, I'd admit it wasn't the first time I'd thought of something like that.

BANG.

A door slammed hard in the hallway. We all looked to one another before scrambling to rush out. Something was happening downstairs. As we rushed down, Rommy held her gloved hands up, so she didn't get the dye on anything.

In the common room, Death barked, "Where's Lucas?" His hands were on Raya's waist, and there was a puddle on the floor.

"What the fuck?" I asked. Rommy and Eve slapped their hands back at me. But only Rommy left a big red handprint on my tee.

She cringed. "Oops, sorry."

"Raya's water's broken," Eve said. Then she gasped. "What do we need to do?"

"Fuckin' find Lucas and get him here."

"He's not here!" a prospect yelled from upstairs. Maybe it was him banging the doors while frantically looking for Lucas.

"Let's relax," Rommy tried.

"No," Death snarled. "Hospital now."

Raya laughed. "Honey, I might not give birth for a while yet."

"What do you mean?" Death demanded.

Raya sighed. "Did you listen to anything in those birthing classes?"

"Sure," the idiot said with a lot of hesitancy.

Raya scowled up at him. "Take me to your room so I can get changed," she demanded just as the kitchen doors swung open and Torch held up a jug of water and tea towels. "This is all I can find."

"What are you gonna do with them?" Rommy asked.

Eve groaned. "It needs to be towels and warm water."

Rommy snickered.

Footsteps pounded down the stairs, and the pale prospect with an armful of towels yelled, "I have towels."

"I'm going to get changed," Raya snapped, but then gripped her belly and moaned, scrunching up her face.

"What? What?" Death demanded.

"Another contraction," Rommy told him. "I'm going to wash my hands." And she headed off to the kitchen like nothing was the matter.

"I'm going to wash my hair out," Eve said.

"Don't leave me," I yelled, but she was already near the stairs and zooming up them.

The prospect moaned, like he was in pain, and sat on the bottom step.

A door opened, and Wrenley raced in. "I'm here." She rushed up to her sister's other side. "That's it. Breathe through it." They both started panting together as Wrenley took Raya's free hand and arm in both of hers.

"Goddamn, if this is what it's like, I don't want any other children," Raya snapped. "Why did we decide this? We should have stuck with not having kids. This shit hurts."

Death looked like he wanted to kill someone for the pain Raya was in. "Not havin' more. This is the only one." He gently brushed her hair from her forehead. "I'd take the pain if I could, darlin'."

She nodded. "I know."

The door behind us slammed open again. "I have him," Saint yelled, running into the room with his brother over his shoulder.

"Zion, I swear I'll let Wade beat you up for this," Lucas snapped, hitting Saint's back.

Wreck stalked into the room as Saint put Lucas on his feet and faced his brother at Raya. "Fix her," he demanded.

Saint dropped his hands from Lucas just as Wreck yanked him back and threw him to the floor. He stood over Saint. "Never fuckin' do that to him again."

"Oh God, here comes another one," Raya let out a pained noise and gripped Wrenley's and Death's arms.

Lucas rushed close. "Someone's water's broken," he commented.

Wreck took in the puddle and blanched. "Fuck." He turned back to Saint and helped him to his feet.

"Damn you and your dick, Leland," Raya snarled.

"Now, darlin'."

"I'm going to cut it off."

Shit. Eve and Rommy aren't having babies.

Wait—

"I'll blend it up and...." She let out a breath and straightened a little. "Okay, that one was rough."

"How far apart are your contractions?" Lucas asked.

"I didn't count," Death said.

Wrenley shook her head.

"That's okay. We'll do it with the next one," Lucas said glancing at his watch.

"I want to get changed," Raya whined.

Lucas smiled. "Then let's go get some other clothes. Do you want me to check how far you're dilated?"

"No," Wreck barked.

"That's doctor business," Death said.

We all looked to Death. I cleared my throat. "You forget Lucas is a doctor?"

"Not one for the pussy," Death clipped.

Jesus.

I wanted to laugh, but then again, if the shoe was on my foot, I'd be uncomfortable about a brother's husband looking between my old lady's legs.

Lucas patted Death's arm. "It's fine. I don't have to. We can get her to the hospital."

Death's jaw clenched, and he nodded.

Raya sighed. "Can I just get changed first?"

Lucas followed as they helped Raya to the stairs where the prospect jumped out of the way, clutching the towels like they were a lifeline.

"I'm back," Rommy announced.

"Raya's gettin' changed and then headin' to the hospital," I told her.

She snorted. "I could hear everything since you all where near shouting." When she got close, she wrapped her hands around my upper arm and shook it. "This is so exciting!"

I screwed up my face. How she thought this was exciting was beyond me. I definitely didn't think it was.

She cackled. "From the look on your face, you don't think so."

"She's in pain, and it made me realise how useless men are when it comes to this type of situation."

"Prospect, clean this," Saint called.

The prospect gagged, covering his mouth with the towels, and shook his head.

Saint glanced to me. "Didn't this kid help clean Snake's knife wound the other day?"

"Yep."

"Why didn't you gag over that, yet you are over a little water?" Saint asked him.

"Then you do it, brother," I said to Saint.

"Fuck off," Saint snapped. "You do it."

My gut rolled. "No way."

Rommy rolled her eyes, laughing. "Prospect, can you grab me a bag, paper towels, and a mop, please?"

He quickly rushed off.

"Thanks, Rommy," I said, reaching out to hook my arm around her neck and give her a side hug.

She rubbed at my back and looked up at me with humour in her gaze. "You know you'll have to do better when it's Eve's turn, right?"

"I—"

"Thank fuck I like dick. Kylo and I ain't havin' kids."

"Where is everyone?" Eve asked as she walked down the stairs with her damp hair.

Rommy told her, "They took Raya upstairs to get changed and then they're taking her to the hospital because Wreck and Death refused to let Lucas look at Raya's vagina."

Eve stopped and then laughed.

The prospect rushed from the kitchen with paper towels and a bag under one arm, while he wheeled the bucket and mop over.

"What's this?" Eve asked, stopping beside Rommy and me. It was then I realised I was still hugging Rommy. I dropped my arm and looked to Eve, but she didn't seem to care.

She just listened to Rommy when she said, "These lot are scared to clean up Raya's juices."

"Rommy, fucking hell, don't say it like that," Saint barked.

As I groaned and pressed a hand to my gut, the prospect gagged again.

Eve cackled along with Rommy.

Rommy took the items from the kid and started cleaning. Eve quickly went to help and asked, "We're heading to the hospital, right?"

Rommy gasped. "Can we? I want to meet the baby after."

They both looked to me. I didn't want to sit around a hospital, but for those two, I would. "Yeah. We'll go."

THE WAITING room was packed with brothers and family. We'd been here for eight hours, and it was nearing midnight. Goddamn made me uneasy thinking that Raya was going through that pain this whole time.

I had Eve and Rommy asleep on each side of me. Both rested their heads on my chest, and I had my arms wrapped around their shoulders.

It was weird at how this wasn't strange.

I enjoyed having both close.

Tech caught my gaze and nodded to both women.

What was he trying to say? I didn't have a clue. I just tipped my chin his way, and he rolled his eyes, smirking, and shaking his head.

It was then Rommy's phone rang.

She sprang up and fumbled it out of her pocket to squint at the screen. She gasped. "Video chat." And she quickly hit Accept. "Hey, hi, hello, bro. Oh look, Mum and Dad are on here too."

Eve stirred and stretched. "What's going on?"

Rommy faced the screen our way. "Video chat."

"Is that our ray of sunshine?" I heard a male voice off to the side of Texas, who sighed, and then someone stole the phone from Rommy's brother. An older man, with greys at his temples, smiled into the screen. "Pumpkin pie, how goes it overseas? Dodge, you handsome man, and the gorgeous as ever Low. When are you three coming home?"

"Very soon, Julian," Low replied.

Rommy showed Eve and me the screen. "Julian, this is Quake and Eve."

"Spank me hard and call me God. They are stunning. Hello, sexy people."

Eve and I grinned and waved.

Julian looked off to somewhere. "You can't have the phone back. I just got it.... Low, your boy is being mean."

Low snorted. "Julian, you know I love you, but we'll see you soon."

Julian sighed. "Fine."

Texas was on the screen again, and he faced the camera to the living room where there was a hell of lot of people.

Rommy leaned close and quietly rattled off some names. "That's Talon. He's the head guy for the Hawks. Next to him is Zara, his woman. That's Coyote, their son, and his woman, Channa. Drake, he's another son, and his woman, Swan. Ruby is a daughter to Talon and Zara, but her man, Dillon, must be working, or he'd be there. Nancy is the grandma, and her man is Gamer. Julian and Mattie."

"All right, quiet please," Texas called. Everyone settled. "Maya has somethin' to tell you."

Zara placed a hand over her mouth.

"We're pregnant," Maya shouted.

Screams started, and most of them jumped up and around congratulating them. Zara stole the phone. "Low, oh my God, we're catching up as soon as you're back."

"We're shopping as soon as I'm back, girl."

Zara grinned. "Totally."

A door opened near the delivery room, and Rommy

gasped as Wrenley stepped out. Rommy quickly said, "Got to go. Love you all, bye," then hung up.

Torch went straight over to his tired-looking woman, supporting her back with his arms around her waist and his nose buried against her neck. He'd hated being away from her for so long.

Wrenley gave us a weary smile. "They've had a healthy baby boy. His name is Phoenix."

Cheers went up, but Eve and Rommy just leaned back against me, both grinning at each other and then up at me.

Christ, they were beautiful.

CHAPTER TWENTY

’d never liked the airport. Not that I’d ever been in one before, even though I had a passport, but I knew it wasn’t a place I’d enjoy. It was too loud and busy. The compound had a heap of people in it, but that was nothing compared to this.

What was worse was the reason I was here. It meant I was losing my friend.

My bottom lip trembled.

Rommy shook her head. “No. Nope. I can’t have you start. If you do, then I will, and it’ll be the end of me. There could be a hot pilot I need to impress, and I can’t do that with snot and tears running down my face.”

My stomach twisted at the thought of Rommy admiring a pilot.

Kayson was hot.

She just needed to look at him. It really didn't bother me if she did.

I just didn't want her to leave.

But I couldn't say that now.

Sniffing, I wiped at my face and nodded. "You'll text me all the time."

She gave me a watery smile. "You'll get sick of how much I'm going to text you."

"Never," I told her.

"Don't forget to give Dusty those recipes you said I should try," Kayson said as he reached out to tap her nose, which she scrunched up.

"I won't, and maybe someday you can both come to see me, and we'll try a heap of things together."

He nodded. "Sounds good."

Don't go, I wanted to shout. *Please don't leave us.*

I gripped Kayson's hand tightly and thinned my lips.

"Goodbyes suck," I said, and my bottom lip trembled again, so I bit down on it. The tears still welled.

Rommy groaned as if in pain. "I can't look at you." She glanced up at Kayson. "Come here, big guy, and give me a hug. I need to get moving to find my parents." They'd already said goodbye to us and left Rommy to do the same.

I didn't want her to go, though.

Kayson released my hand and picked Rommy up, swaying her side to side as he hugged her tightly. His jaw clenched, like he was fighting his emotions too. But then I saw him nod, so I knew Rommy was telling him something.

Shouldn't I be jealous over that?

Over seeing him gently kiss her cheek and temple?

I had no idea, other than I wasn't.

I thought it sweet, cute, and even sexy.

My heart pounded at the idea of seeing them kiss, but more so over me touching my lips to Rommy's.

It was obvious Kayson cared about her, maybe even as much as I did. We'd all grown so close. But on what level did we care? Why was I thinking about kissing her? Why did I want my boyfriend to?

Now she was leaving.

To another part of the world.

So far away.

Too far away.

Kayson nodded again before he gave her one last kiss on the temple. She patted his back before he set her back on her feet.

When she stepped away with tears streaming down her face, my own dam burst.

"You weren't supposed to cry," I wailed as we reached out at the same time to hug each other. I buried my face into the crook of her neck and felt her running a hand over my hair.

Don't go. Please.

I want you here.

Stay with us.

But I couldn't do that to her, not when I didn't know exactly *how* I wanted her to stay—as a friend or more. It was selfish to think about all this as she was leaving. I needed to work myself out before anything.

"The best thing about being kidnapped was meeting you and Quake. You're a sweet, wonderful, gorgeous person, Eve, and never think badly of yourself again because I love the woman you are, and if I hear you say unkind things about yourself, I'm going to have to slap you silly. Don't be mean to *my* person." Her voice cracked, and she cleared her throat.

I whined, shaking my head, unable to form words.

"Take care of your big guy. The love you have for each other is something special, and I know it's going to be amazing." She gave me one last squeeze before stepping back.

When I started to reach for her, she smiled sadly and moved out of reach. Kayson curled an arm around my waist, holding me in place.

Rommy grinned, new tears welling as she sent us the peace sign. "You two are the best people in the universe. Later, gators." Then she turned and rushed through the crowd.

Kayson kissed my shoulder. "It'll be okay."

Would it?

Why did it feel like my heart was being crushed?

When I heard his sniff, I turned in his arms and looked up at him.

Oh God. My beautiful man had tears in his eyes too.

He gave me a tight smile and shrugged. "I ain't immune to all the tears you two produced."

Cupping his cheeks, I went to my toes and kissed him before wrapping my arms around him. "Goodbyes suck," I said again.

"Fuck yes they do."

I wanted to drag Kayson with me to go find her.

We had to keep her here with us.

Kidnap her ourselves.

Because something already felt like it was missing.

QUAKE

LOCK IT DOWN.

Lock it the fuck down.

Clenching my jaw, I hugged Eve to me.

Rommy's words played on my mind.

"I know you'll love her with everything you have because you're a good man, Quake. You and Eve mean so much to me, and I'm going to miss you both like crazy. Take care of each other while we're apart, you smart, smoking-hot man."

I hadn't even laughed at her words. I'd been too choked up to say anything.

I wanted to tell her she meant a lot to us, too, but I couldn't even do that.

Rommy was now gone. She'd be going through security and then getting on a plane back to Australia.

It didn't sit right with me.

Eve was struggling too. The tears from all of us were enough of a sign. They weren't for just a friend either. Rommy had made a place in my heart and Eve's. She was lodged, stuck, and seeing her walk away was fucking hard.

It hollowed my gut.

I wanted to pick Eve up and carry her with me to go after Rommy, then grab Rommy under my other arm and take them both home.

Fuck.

This shit wasn't right.

My chest goddamn ached.

But it was too late.

She was gone.

And it really wasn't right to try and figure out if the two of us could become three. Eve had only just accepted me. It'd be so wrong of me to suggest that our feelings for Rommy were something stronger than friendship.

Eve would have to figure it out for herself without my help.

If she ever did.

ROMANIA

CUSTOMS WAS JUST around the corner. I had to keep it together for now. I had to get through to my parents and then I could shatter. I wanted to stay. I wanted to be with them, but they didn't see me as anything other than a friend.

With my head down, I turned the corner and thumped into a chest.

I looked up into Dad's sad eyes. His hand dropped to the top of my head. "Kid?"

I shook my head.

"You can let it go," he told me.

Again, I shook my head, jaw clenched, tears welling.

If I let go, I wouldn't be able to stop, and I'd be a mess through security, and they'd think I was a drug lord or a bomber or something.

Dad cupped the back of my head. "You're always a strong, brave woman, Rom. But it's okay to let go. Who gives a flying fuck about anyone else seein' my daughter lettin' her emotions ride her. They mean a lot to you, darlin'. Let it go, Rom."

My face crumbled, and I pushed in against Dad's chest, crying, *sobbing*.

It's not fair.

It's not fair.

It's not fair.

I was supposed to find love that could last forever and get to keep it, not have to walk away from it.

It wasn't fair.

I just wanted them to care about me like I did them.

But I couldn't have them.

I couldn't keep them.

They weren't mine.

"Oh, sweetie," Mum whispered from beside me and then I felt her hugging my back. "They mean something big to you, don't they?"

I nodded against Dad's chest.

"One day they'll realise what they lost."

Sniffing, I wiped at my face and shook my head. "I-I have to let them go. They... they don't need me messing up their love."

Wiping at my face again, I swallowed thickly and forced my emotions down. Still, my eyes welled again so I scrubbed at them. "I'm okay. I-I'll be okay." The tears wouldn't quit, though, and my parents' stare had me thinking that they thought I was the biggest liar in the world.

Which I was.

It hurts.

So much.

My chest burned.

They'd stolen a part of my heart, but they didn't do it on purpose. They didn't know my heart wanted to stay with them.

I was just their friend.

That was all I'd ever be.

Sniffing again, I rubbed more tears away. "I'm okay." I gave them a watery smile.

Dad's jaw clenched. "You're not, but it's okay to be heartbroken, kid. Your mum and I weren't blind when it came to you placin' your feelin's in their palms. They're fools for not seein' the way you felt."

I scowled, but I was still leaking and swiping the tears away. "They aren't fools. They're the best people ever. Don't be a dick, Dad."

He snorted and cupped the back of my head to drag me against him again. "Okay, kid. I'll try not to be."

"Thank you," I cried, gripping his tee under his cut.

One day it wouldn't hurt as much, but for now, I'd allow the pain to take me under. They really did mean so much to me.

I love them.

CHAPTER TWENTY-ONE

THE THREE STOOGES GROUP CHAT

ROMMY:

> Just landed. You guys are probably asleep. It's raining here, which matches my mood. I miss the Diamond MC compound already.

QUAKE:

> Eve just drifted off, but I've been gaming. Good to see you made it back safely. The compound misses you too.

ROMMY:

> Hey, Quake. What are you playing? We'll have to get online and play together some time.

QUAKE:

I'm down for that. Just let me know when you're free. Time differences will be shit, though. Currently playing Call of Duty. Well, I was. Might hit the sack now.

ROMMY:

Cool cool. I'll talk to you soon. Hugs to you both!!!!

QUAKE:

You too, Rommy.

EVE:

I'm bored.

ROMMY:

Wish I was there to help. I'm just about to start work.

EVE:

How is it being back now?

ROMMY:

Busy. I'm booked up every day.

EVE:

> I'll let you get started then.

ROMMY:

Eve, is there a tone implied here? You know I'd talk to you over anything or anyone, right? I'm just telling you I've been busy at work, but it doesn't mean I don't want to talk to you. Ever.

EVE:

> Sorry. I took it wrong. I should know you're not like that. I miss having you around. Kayson misses you too. He tries to get me to try different foods. I need you back to save me.

ROMMY:

Ha-ha, poor you. Try the food, Eve. Don't be a chicken.

EVE:

ROMMY:

Ha-ha. Sorry, babe, I have to talk to a customer. Text as soon as I can x

QUAKE:

Did you steal my vintage Guns and Roses tee? You eyed it off and threatened to take it and now I can't find it.

ROMMY:

Me? I would never.

EVE:

LOL! She totally did. Good work, Rommy.

QUAKE:

I'll get it back one day.

ROMMY:

That's if I took it and Eve's black hoodie.

EVE:

WTH? We're supposed to gang up on Kayson. You're not supposed to work on your own.

ROMMY:

Sometimes a girl needs to have her own evil plans.

QUAKE:

You could never be evil.

EVE:

> I agree with Kayson.

QUAKE:

> See, I'm right all the time.

EVE:

> Don't get ahead of yourself.

ROMMY:

> I can kick butt and be evil when I need to be.

EVE:

> True. But still, you're our ray of sunshine who we miss terribly.

QUAKE:

> What Eve said.

ROMMY:

> Awww, guys. I miss you two every day.

> No every hour.

> No every second of every hour and all the days.

> Miss you two a LOT.

QUAKE:

> Eve's crying now.

EVE:

> I am not. Shut up.

ROMMY:

Are you two seriously sitting next to
each other texting me? I feel special.

QUAKE:

> You are.

EVE:

Yes, we are. Just having brekkie
together.

ROMMY:

Ha, I see what you did there shortening
the word like I do. I've rubbed off on
you. Love it!

ROMMY SENDS PHOTO OF HERSELF IN A LITTLE BLACK DRESS.

ROMMY:

Hey, hi, hello. I'm just about to head out
the door for the club. How do I look?

EVE:

No.

QUAKE:

Fuck no.

ROMMY:

Not short enough? HA-HA. What do you mean no?

EVE:

Where are you going?

QUAKE:

Who are you going with?

EVE:

I have to walk into work. Kayson, you deal with this.

QUAKE:

How??????

ROMMY:

You guys crack me up. I'm going to a club to drink and dance with some friends.

QUAKE:

Are these Hawks friends?

ROMMY:

No. They're kidnappee friends.

ROMMY SENDS PHOTO OF HER, CAL, JENNY, IOLA, AND THEIR BOYFRIENDS.

ROMMY:

Pre-drinks at my place before we
head out.

QUAKE:

Who're all the guys?

Actually, I want all names. First and last
names and their addresses.

What's the club you're going to? Do your
parents know?

ROMMY:

OMG do you need me to call you
Daddy too?

....

....

ROMMY:

Have I broken you? HA-HA.

ROMMY:

Sorry, Eve. I broke your man. I've got to go. Love you both xxxxxxxxx

QUAKE:

Text us as soon as you get there and get home, Rommy xx

ROMMY:

EVE:

Kayson is PISSED.

ROMMY:

It's too early. And why?

EVE:

You didn't text when you got home. He called your dad to make sure you were in your bed.

ROMMY:

No way! What happens if I had a guy in
my room and my dad walked in?

EVE:

Well, it's lucky you didn't and were
passed out alone instead.

ROMMY:

I'm going to die a spinster with cats and
a house that smells like cat pee.

EVE:

No, you won't. You'll be snapped up
because you're amazing.

ROMMY:

Thanks, babe. I'm gonna nap for a bit. It
was a late night.

EVE:

Talk soon xx

ROMMY:

Of course xx

ROMMY:

Anyone have time for a game?

QUAKE:

I'm not talking to you.

ROMMY:

Aww, you still mad? I can't help forgetting things when I'm drunk. I could hardly see my hands let alone work out how to use my phone.

QUAKE:

You shouldn't be that drunk in the first place.

EVE:

Rommy's getting scolded.

ROMMY:

Usually I like a bit of spanking while that happens.

EVE:

Kayson can do that too.

....

EVE:

Ha-ha, I broke Rommy.

QUAKE:

> I'm at the bar, and it's packed. Can't text right now, but I'm down for the spanking xx

ROMMY:

If only I'd known you two were this kinky before I left xx

EVE:

> If only. Sorry, Rommy. I have to babysit Seth so Dusty and Country can have a date night. I'll text when I can xx

CHAPTER TWENTY-TWO

EVE

Even three weeks later I still couldn't stop thinking about Rommy. I'd let her leave without actually trying to see if there was something more between us?

As in the three of us.

I needed to talk with Kayson about my thoughts of Rommy joining us.

Thoughts that had recently taken a turn into a dirtier fantasy that made me horny as hell.

Thoughts of Rommy kissing Kayson and then me.

Rommy naked and riding Kayson while I watched and touched myself.

Of both Rommy and I sharing Kayson's cock as we sucked, licked, and swallowed his seed.

My mouth watered and belly swooped at the thought of tasting her or having her between my legs.

Yet, I was still a little scared that Kayson would think that this would be cheating.

Then again, I was jumping to the worst-case scenario without giving him a chance to say he understood because he liked her too. I really did believe he had feelings for her but never said anything because he was worried what *I* would think.

Or was that just me hoping?

Kayson was an understanding guy and a man who liked to talk things out before they became a problem.

Not that Rommy was a problem.

I just couldn't stop thinking about her and wondering that if we did try, it could be something amazing.

Not that what I had with Kayson wasn't already.

Oh God. I was a bad person for being attracted to someone else when I'd finally committed to the man I loved and hoped he was into another woman too.

You're useless, pathetic. No one will love you.

That wasn't true, though.

"Sweetheart?"

I jumped up from the couch, wringing my hands together. "I'm sorry."

He stopped and stilled. "For what?"

It was then I burst into tears and buried my face into my hands, my nerves and anxiety getting the better of me.

Next, I was up in his arms before he sat on the couch with me straddling his lap as he held me against his chest.

"What's wrong, sweetheart? Did I do somethin'? Did someone say somethin'? I'll kick their fuckin' ass if anyone upset you."

In the crook of his neck and shoulder, I shook my head. "No one upset me, but myself."

"How?" He rubbed his hands up and down my back.

I couldn't tell him.

The words were stuck in my throat.

Fear of losing him made me sick to the stomach.

I wouldn't jeopardise what we had. I'd just got him.

"Eve, sweetheart. I'm going to take a guess, and if I'm totally off base, hit me for it."

He couldn't guess.

Not unless he'd already thought of it too.

Not unless he was as lost as I was without Rommy here.

We had each other and were amazing together, but Rommy was ours too.

Leaning back, I sniffed and wiped at my face as I nodded.

Gently, he brushed his thumb over my cheek and smiled softly. "You're missin' Rommy?"

I nodded.

"But it's in a different way than you'd miss Dusty or Courtney."

Again, I nodded.

"I'm missin' her in the same way."

My eyes widened.

"Can you imagine kissin' her?" he asked.

"Yes," I whispered. "And her kissing you."

"Can you imagine doin' other things with her?" he asked, studying my face so he saw my blush.

"Naked things?" I managed to get out.

"Yeah, sweetheart."

"Yes," I admitted. "But this isn't cheating. I'd never. I want all of us to do these things together. No one gets left out, and that's only if we believe something could grow between the three of us. But it's not cheating. I wouldn't."

He cupped my cheeks and pulled me close. "I know it ain't cheatin', sweetheart. I know you nor I would do that to each other. And if somethin' does happen between the three of us, it doesn't mean I don't love you any different. You're stuck with me for the rest of our lives. Nothin' will change between us."

I sagged against him, the tension draining from my body.

He hugged me tightly. "You were stressin' about tellin' me this?"

"Yeah," I breathed.

"We ain't your parents, sweetheart. We know our love is strong and will last for-fuckin'-ever, but it'll just include another."

When Kayson and I had been in bed the other night, I'd told him about my parents and what Tech and I had gone through with them and then later on the streets. He'd held me through it all and promised that my life would just get better.

With my cheek to his chest, I played with the edge of his cut. "You have feelings for Rommy?"

"Seeing the way she supported you and spendin' time with her, it was hard not to have somethin' grow. That's why we're talkin' about this now, right? You want us to try and be a throuple? The three of us datin' and seein' if it'll lead to marriage and all the other stuff?"

Lifting myself up, I smiled softly. "I'd like exactly that. You?"

"Yeah, sweetheart. You and Rommy have my heart."

My belly fluttered. Leaning against him, I asked, "Can you picture Rommy and I kissing?"

His hands gripped at my bare thighs. I was glad I wore shorts to feel them better. He cleared this throat. "Yeah."

"Can you picture Rommy kissing you?"

He nodded.

Scraping my top teeth over my bottom lip, I toyed with the neck of his tee as I asked, "Can you picture me going down on Rommy?"

"Fuck," he drew out. "Can you? Is it somethin' you'd do?"

Smirking, I shrugged. "I'd like to try."

"I'm sure she'd be up for you testin' it out."

Laughing, I nodded. "I think you'd be right."

His hands clenched against my skin. "I can also picture you between her legs while I'm fuckin' you from behind and watchin' you and her drive each other wild."

Moaning, I kissed his neck. "I want that."

"We'll make it happen."

"But first, I want you to fuck me right now."

His hands slid to my ass and gripped. "I can do that. Bed?"

I shook my head and licked up to his ear where I sucked his lobe into my mouth. He groaned and rocked up against my damp shorts.

"Here. Need you in me."

"Christ, sweetheart." His hands moved between my legs. There was a tug and then a rip.

I jerked back. "Did you just rip my shorts?"

He grinned. "Yep." His fingers slid under my panties, and there was another tear. "You have more."

Laughing, I nodded. Leaning in, I kissed him with a slow dance of our tongues. His fingers glided into my wet pussy, and I moaned into his mouth. A thumb ran over my clit, making me shudder. Pleasure rolled down my spine.

Breaking the kiss, I dropped my forehead to his shoulder. "Kayson."

"Nice and wet for me, sweetheart. Fuckin' love that."

Panting, I hummed before I said, "I bet Rommy would be as wet."

"Jesus," he hissed, his fingers fucking me faster.

"Yeah, she'd love your cock like I do. We could suck and lick it together while you wrap your fists into our hair to guide us."

I lost his fingers so he could make quick work of undoing his jeans before he lifted me to thrust his cock deep inside. I arched back and moaned from the full feeling his cock gave me.

"Such a good cock," I breathed.

His hand gripped my neck, and he demanded, "Ride me."

Smiling, I reached behind to hold his knees and lifted myself up before bouncing down again. Over and over, I fucked his cock in and out of me.

His other hand swept up under my tee to my bare breast. He pinched and tugged at my nipple, making me whimper.

"Rommy could be here standing on the couch between us. You could lick and bite at her ass, and I'd do the same to her pussy."

His growl was almost animalistic, and I loved it.

His other hand tightened around my neck.

I pushed into his touch, moaning and then gasping for

air when he cut off my oxygen. Blood pumped hard, and I knew my face would be bright red. He took control, drilling up into me.

God, I loved this man.

He released my throat, and I gasped, then panted until I had enough air into my deprived lungs.

Opening my eyes, I smirked. "You loved that idea."

"Yes," he hissed.

"I'd love to see you fuck her, Kayson. Like you are me. I want her face red from your hand on her throat, and I'd still make her kiss me. Then I'd sit over her face and—"

"Jesus Christ, sweetheart," he bit out. "I ain't gonna last if you keep talkin' like that."

Laughing, I went back riding him as he settled back against the couch. "I love that you like it. Love that your heart is big enough for both of us."

"Fuckin' love you, Eve. Love that you were brave to tell me your thoughts and want to test the waters. We'll see where this all goes."

I hummed and nodded. "Yes."

He hooked a hand at the back of my neck and drew me in. Slanting his mouth to mine, he kissed me as I kept fucking his beautiful cock.

His hands cupped my ass, one slid closer to my crack, and he traced a finger over my hole before he tapped it. He'd fucked me there a couple of times, and I'd loved it.

Nipping at his bottom lip, I told him, "Next time I want you to fuck me there. Mark me with your cum."

"Fuck yes, sweetheart."

A tingle rolled down my spine at the memory of Kayson eating my ass. He enjoyed playing with all areas of my body.

"Kayson," I whimpered. "Close."

His jaw clenched, and he nodded, resting his forehead to mine. He hands went back to my waist as he guided me up and down his dick.

Pleasure slammed into me. "Kayson," I cried, coming and clamping over his gliding cock.

He groaned low. "Fuck." His cum rushed out, warming me in ways that were perfect.

I rested against him, his cock still inside me. Kissing his neck, I breathed, "Love you."

He hugged me tightly to him, his dick twitching inside. "Fuckin' love you, Eve."

"Are you sure?"

"As sure as I am about you and me. It'll be somethin' to work through and figure out, but the three of us can do it. We're already close in so many ways, and I think sex will bring the bond we're creating to somethin' extraordinary."

Smiling, I toyed with his hair at the back of his neck. "How are we going to bring this up with her?"

His hand ran up under my tee to my bare back. "I think it'll be best to do it in person."

Gasping, I sat up. "Are you saying we're going to Australia?"

He grinned. "We're going to Australia."

CHAPTER TWENTY-THREE

ROMANIA

"**K**id, you good?" Dad asked, resting his hand on my neck and giving me a little shake.

I placed my phone down on the counter in the garage break room and shrugged. "Eve and Quake haven't got back to me in forever."

Dad smirked. "Forever?"

"I don't know. They're acting weird. Maybe they don't want to talk to me anymore. Maybe they just want to concentrate on each other. Not that I can blame them. Their relationship's new. They don't need me annoying them all the time with messages or calls or FaceTime."

"I'm sure that's not the case."

I scoffed. "I've had people get sick of me in my life, Dad. It wouldn't surprise me."

He glared. "Fuck those people, kid. The friendship you

have with Eve and Quake was somethin' big. They're probably just busy or somethin'."

I hummed. "I guess. But neither of them has messaged me in like... hours. Right now, it'll be evening there, and they'd be having dinner, or Quake would be getting ready to go to the bar, and Eve would either go with him or stay home to chat with me. But no one is talking to me." Sighing, I scrubbed a hand over my face and then took a deep breath. "I'm overreacting. You're probably right. They're just busy."

Too busy for me.

I shouldn't be surprised. I couldn't expect them to keep talking to me when they should be working on their relationship.

"Rommy—"

Pushing my shoulders back, I smiled up at Dad. "Nope. I'm all good. They'll text sooner or later. I'm gonna grab a strawberry milk and head to my bay. I have a sweet car waiting for me."

Dad thinned his lips, but he nodded. "Okay, kid. Good to keep busy."

"Exactly." On my way out, I took a carton of strawberry milk out of the refrigerator. Not that I really wanted it. I wasn't in the mood for a drink or food, but I didn't want to worry Dad more. I still opened it and drank it down before throwing it in one of the rubbish bins along the way.

"Rommy, you comin' to see Payton in her school concert?" Billy asked as I walked by his bay where he and Pick were tinkering on their rides.

"When was it again?" I asked, smiling sheepishly. Things slipped my mind all the time, and I even forget to put it in my calendar to remind me.

"Next weekend."

"Text me a link to the tickets. Is she singing?" Payton had an amazing voice, and I believed she could go far with it, if her dads let go of the reins. I'd have to talk to Josie to see if she thought Payton wanted a career in music.

"Yeah, got the main role in *Hairspray*."

"Oh my God, I love that movie. I'll be there."

Pick tipped his chin up at me smiling as Billy said, "Wicked."

I kept moving on to my bay. Knife and Beast weren't in yet. They probably had a late one since there'd been a party at the club. I hadn't gone. I'd worked my butt off yesterday and went home to see if Quake and Eve were free to chat, but they never got back to me.

Had I done something?

Maybe I said the wrong thing.

I tended to do that a lot.

But I thought they didn't mind me being me.

They could just be busy.

But we'd never gone this long without talking in one way or another.

If they'd just sent one quick text, I wouldn't be all up in my head with worry or fear that I'd lost them.

I couldn't lose them.

In my bay, I slipped on my coveralls and grabbed my headphones.

Please let my work and music take my mind off everything else.

I just needed a breather from the achy chest and twisted gut.

Placing my headphones on, I selected a playlist and busied myself with the job.

I loved my work.

It was a puzzle most days, and it did entertain my mind.

Except today, I kept glancing at my phone to see if the screen was lit up with a new message.

It wasn't, and the minutes were dragging by painfully.

Once again, I shoved my mind back onto business. This time I lasted another hour before I picked up my phone.

Groaning, I put the device down and felt a tap on my shoulder.

I jolted and paused the music to meet Knife's amused gaze. "Sorry to startle, kid. Dodge wants you in the compound."

I glanced back to the bike. "But I've got to get this finished." I didn't tell him I'd wasted enough time looking at my phone instead of working. He didn't need to know that.

"I'll get Fang to finish it off." He nodded to the side. "We'll tell him on the way."

Sighing, I placed my headphones on the counter, ticked off what I'd completed, and then removed my coveralls, which left me in jeans and a plain black tee. I slipped my boots back on and nodded. "Okay." As we walked, I asked, "Do you know what he wants?"

Shit. I hope I didn't mess up on any of the jobs. I prided myself on my work. If I got a complaint right now, I'd likely burst into tears and have the brothers running for cover while I sorted myself out. Then again, I didn't think I could sort myself out until I heard from Eve and Quake.

"Nah, don't have a clue. Sorry."

"How come he's not in the office in the garage anyway?"

"Again, you're askin' me somethin' I don't have an answer to." He spotted Fang and called, "Brother, can you finish up for Rommy."

Fang tipped his chin up. "No problem. You marked off on the form what's been done and hasn't?"

"Sure did." The forms were what Mum had made up to help me on days when my mind was a buzz and nothing would settle it. "Thanks, Fang."

"Any time," he called as he walked towards my bay.

Knife and I moved on, and he asked, "You all right, Rom?"

"Yeah, why?" I pulled one of the braids over my shoulder to play with the end.

He bumped his arm into mine. "You just don't seem yourself."

Sighing, I nodded. "My mind is elsewhere. But I'll be fine." I smiled up at him.

"Yeah, I reckon you will," he told me as he opened the door to the compound.

We walked down the hall that led to the common room where I could hear Dad talking to someone. Did we have guests he wanted me to meet?

Oh hell, imagine if he was trying to set me up with someone.

He'd never tried that on me before, but he could tell I wasn't 100 percent happy when my heart was still at the Diamond MC compound.

Actually, I doubted he'd be that silly to ever try to set me up.

He knew I'd give him a piece of my mind, and I wouldn't wait for a quiet time to do it.

Turning the corner, I stopped.

My heart jumped into my throat, and I covered my mouth with one hand while I gripped my tee at my chest with the other.

It was a hallucination.

I'd gone and lost it and was now seeing things.

They couldn't be real.

They wouldn't be here.

Why was I seeing Eve and Quake in the Hawks Motorcycle Club compound?

"Kid," Dad said.

With a shaky hand, I pointed to the ones who had stolen my heart. "Are they real?"

Chuckles started, and Eve gave me a watery smile as she nodded while Quake just grinned big.

"Sorry we didn't text back," Quake said.

"We were busy getting here," Eve added.

Like an idiot, I dropped to my knees, bent over, and started crying.

Heavy footsteps rushed towards me. I was picked up by an arm around my waist, and as soon as I had my feet to the floor, Eve was there tugging my hands from my face.

"Rommy?"

"I-I thought you hated me. I thought you both had enough and wanted to stop talking to me."

"Fuck," Quake clipped from behind me. He touched his chin to my shoulder. "Never."

Eve cupped my cheeks and stepped closer. "Kayson's right. We'd never stop talking to you or hate you or have enough of you." She smiled softly as she gently swiped my tears away. "Why do you think we're here?"

I whimpered and shrugged.

Did I forget something?

"We can't stay away," Quake said.

My eyes widened, and Eve nodded before she told me, "We missed you like crazy, Rommy."

"I missed you guys too," I cried, then buried my face into Eve's chest. "Sandwich me," I demanded. They both let out a laugh, as did the others, but Eve and Quake squished me between them.

"How long are you here for?" I asked.

Already I dreaded their answer, knowing it would be too soon, and they'd leave me again.

"We'll figure that out," Quake said.

"Rommy," Eve said softly. I lifted my head from her chest to meet her warm gaze that searched my face before she looked over my head to Quake. "I don't think she gets it."

He grunted. "Me either. Show her, sweetheart."

Show me what?

As Eve smiled, her gaze shifted back to me, and she cupped my cheeks before slowly moving her head closer.

Holy fuck. Her gaze was locked on my lips.

This can't be real.

It can't be.

And yet, Eve pressed her lips to mine in a gentle caress before pulling back.

I blinked. "You kissed me."

Eve smirked. "I did."

"*You* kissed me," I said again to make sure she knew she really had, and it wasn't a mistake.

"I know."

Looking over my shoulder, I told Quake like he wasn't there to witness it, "Eve kissed *me*."

He grinned. "Saw that." Then *he* leaned down and pressed his lips to mine in a quick peck.

My heart thundered.

A shiver of arousal raced down my spine.

They were here for me.

Right?

When Quake lifted his head, I glanced to both and told them, "Kissing me is like claiming me. Once you've done it, there are no take backs."

More chuckles sounded.

But Eve and Quake just grinned at me.

Quake's hands rubbed up and down my sides. He kissed my neck and then Eve's lips. "That's what we're hopin' for."

Gasping, I moved from between them and asked, "Are you completely sure? I'm a lot. You know that, but if you're around me all the time, then it can get too much."

"Bullshit," Eve snapped.

"Ain't true," Quake said at the same time.

"Damn right," Dad commented.

"But—"

"No." Eve shook her head and took my hand in both of hers to hold them against her chest. "You told me not to listen to those thoughts I have about myself, and I want the same from you, Rommy. You're an amazing, beautiful soul, who is a pleasure to be around all the damn time."

"Know it didn't help us not textin' you, little devil, but we're here in front of you to show you that you mean a fuckin' load to us, and we want somethin' to work between the three of us." Quake kissed my cheek. "You willin' to try with us?"

"You want that?"

"We do," Eve said.

Taking Quake's hand in mine, I leaned into Eve and slanted my mouth over hers. She whimpered into the kiss, opening up to my tongue as they danced around. With a final peck, I then turned and gripped the back of Quake's neck to yank him down and kiss him with as much heat and want as I did Eve.

My body hummed.

I had them here.

I'd kissed them both.

They wanted something with me.

ME!

They wanted me.

I wasn't sure how this would work out, but I was willing to put my all into making sure this relationship would work.

Call me a grade-A student when it comes to these two.

CHAPTER TWENTY-FOUR

EVE

As first kisses went with a woman, I could say I was all on board to do it again and again and again. Even watching Rommy and Kayson making out flooded me with heat.

Biting my bottom lip, I wished we were somewhere else.

A place we could be alone.

Thankfully, we'd called Dodge and Low about us flying over. We'd had time for a shower and change of clothes to wash the plane ride away before we saw Rommy. It also meant we could have Rommy for the day since they'd made sure she was covered with work.

At the thought of the phone call with Rommy's parents, I smiled.

Nerves fluttered my stomach as I watched Quake put his phone on speaker while it rang and rang.

"Since it's mornin' here, I'm gonna think that you're not checkin' on Rommy at a club," Dodge answered.

Kayson and I shared a look, and I waved frantically for him to say something while he gave me wide eyes.

It was then I realised it would've been great if we'd planned what we were going to say instead of just jumping the gun.

There was a sigh before Dodge asked, "I can hear two people breathin' so I'm guessin' Eve's there too. Please fuckin' tell me you two have pulled your heads out of your arses to see that Rommy is someone amazin' you can't do without?"

Kayson and I stared at each other. I swallowed thickly and said, "Yes?"

"You don't sound certain."

Kayson quickly added, "We are. It's just new, but we want to make sure, which is why we're comin' to Australia."

"And if I said stay the fuck away from her?" he asked.

"No," I blurted. "Sorry, but we can't, and I don't think she'd want us to either."

He grunted. "Text me your flight details, I'll have a couple of brothers pick you two up. Names are Knife and Beast. I'll make sure she gets away from work, but you come to the compound. I need to see that my girl wants this."

Now I was certain Dodge understood that Rommy wanted this with us. She was willing to try.

When Kayson pulled back, they both smiled at each other, and it warmed my heart.

"We're gonna steal you away for the day," Kayson told her.

She spun around to her father, and he said, "Your mum

and I have already cleared your schedule. The brothers are takin' on your clients while they're in town."

My belly rolled.

Kayson and I'd eventually go back to America. Would Rommy want to come with us or... could Kayson and I live in Australia with her?

It was something we'd have to figure out.

The step we'd taken with coming here, though, to add Rommy into the relationship, was the right choice to make. I knew it to the very tips of my toes. Rommy was meant to be with us.

Since she'd left, there was a Rommy-sized hole in our lives.

What Kayson and I already had was amazing, but I believed adding Rommy would take us to a new level. One that would be full of love, life, and laughs.

Rommy clapped and danced on the spot, beaming at me. "While you're here, I can take you both to so many places. We'll have so much to do and talk about, and... Gah. I'm overwhelmed with happiness." She hugged us again. "You're here. You're really here for *me*." Her voice broke.

"Everyone out," Dodge called, and people vacated the common room quickly.

Before Dodge and Low left with the others, Low walked by us with a watery gaze. "Thank you," she mouthed.

While I nodded, Kayson tipped his chin up before he surrounded us both with his big body, and I held Rommy tightly to me.

I whispered just for her and Kayson, "We couldn't go another day without seeing you. The texts weren't enough. The calls or seeing you through a screen was never enough."

"We'll figure out where this is gonna go, but we needed to come in person to let you know you mean a fuckin' lot to us, Rommy," Kayson said before he kissed us both on the head.

She sniffed and lifted her gaze. Tears brimmed, but she was grinning big. "Walking away from you two broke my heart, but today, you've both healed it again. You both care about me and knowing that couldn't make me happier. I know it's weird and strange, and I don't expect anything back, but the time I spent with you two was the best in my life. I knew the love I had for you two is ginormous. Fills me up each and every time I think of you both, and that's a lot. Like a lot." She nodded.

She loves us.

She said it.

Kayson's fingers slid into her hair, and he stared down at her with an intense gaze before he roughly asked her, "You love us?"

"With everything I have, and I'm sorry if it's too much and—"

I pressed two fingers to her lips. "We travelled the world to get to you because you hold a piece of our hearts in you. Having you gone with those pieces dimmed our world. You belong with us, Rommy. Kayson and I love each other so much, but our love extends to you too."

"Shit," she snapped before burying her face again to cry. We just held her tighter.

Kayson leaned down and kissed the back of her neck. "Eve's right. You have our love, little devil."

"You guys!" she cried, lifting her face and wiping at it as

she took a step away. "I can't stop leaking. I'm just so happy."

"Have at it then, Rom," Kayson said.

"I'm glad they're happy tears, Rommy."

She let out a strangled laugh. "You both love me."

We smiled, and I said, "We do."

"That means, when I don't have tears and snot all over my face, I can kiss you both."

Kayson chuckled. "Yeah, Rommy. You can."

"I want to do more too," she announced. "Since you guys love me." It was like she couldn't believe we did and had to keep saying the words. Not that we minded. We'd reassure her all the time if we had to.

Kayson winked. "We're down for doin' more."

Her gaze swung to me. "Eve, are you comfortable?"

"With you, I believe anything is possible."

When a strangled moan escaped her, she covered her face. "Too sweet."

I noticed some napkins on a table and pointed them out to Kayson. While he went and got some, I moved up beside Rommy to trace my hand over her back.

A door opened, and a tall guy with facial hair stomped in. He stopped and took in Rommy crying. "What the fuck is goin' on?"

"Hi, I'm—"

"Rommy, kid, you good? Did they do somethin'? Want me to kick their arses? Where the hell is everyone? Don't move another muscle towards them, big guy. You might be a mammoth, but I can still fuck you up."

Rommy laughed. "Dive." She wiped at her face and sniffed up.

Kayson kept walking back to us.

"Don't move," Dive clipped. He picked up a chair, like he was going to throw it at Kayson, and I stopped breathing. I didn't want to hurt anyone in Rommy's family, but I'd put a stop to it somehow before he got close to Kayson. Hell, I'd even do the same for Rommy if anyone in the Diamond MC threatened her with a chair.

"Oh my God," Rommy breathed, stepping in front of me as she laughed again. "Love you, Dive, but don't threaten my people." Kayson handed Rommy the napkins.

Dive placed the chair down. "Your people? These two the reason you've been mopey, kid?"

After she blew her nose and wiped at her face, she glared. "I haven't been mopey."

He scoffed. "Yeah, okay."

"Dive," she whined. "Stop being a dick and meet my people."

He grinned, then looked at both of us. "Hey." He tipped his chin up. "Name's Dive, and if either of you fuck Rommy over, I'm gonna be the one rippin' you apart, then burying—"

"Dive," Rommy snapped, but added, "It's really nice you want to murder on my behalf, but Eve and Quake won't hurt me."

He huffed. "They'd fuckin' better not."

Kayson stepped forward. "Appreciate you lookin' out for Rommy. I know you and the club will keep doin' it, but you won't be the only ones. Rommy not only grabbed our hearts"—he pointed at me and himself—"but she has the brothers of the Diamond MC too. We'll make sure nothin' in the world can hurt her. Even when we have to protect her from herself when she tries to pick a fight with an ex-mafia man."

Dive's gaze flared before he guffawed. "What? Dodge didn't tell me that."

"Tell you what?" Dodge asked as he and Low reentered.

"About your monster wantin' to fight an ex-mafia guy."

Dodge grinned. "At the time we didn't know he had ties to the Russian mafia."

"*Russian* mafia?" Dive yelled. He lasered Rommy with a scowl. "What the fuck were you thinkin', kid?"

Rommy groaned. "I could take him."

Dive stared at her, then glared at Dodge. "See what you two created?" He faced Kayson and me. "Good luck. You're both gonna need it."

"Hey!" Rommy snapped.

I walked up to Rommy and took her hand. She looked down at it and then smiled at me before she leaned in and kissed me quickly.

"I can do that now," she said.

"You can."

"You just tell me if there's anything I do to you that you don't like—"

"Kid, how about you take Eve and Quake back to the house?" Dodge said quickly, then added something that had my cheeks blushing, "Your mum and I are gonna stay in our room here."

Rommy bounced around on her feet and shot her dad finger guns. "Good thinking, old man. We gotta test these waters to see if us three will click in the—"

"Fuck's sake, Rom." Dodge dropped his head back and sighed long and loud before he straightened and continued,

"Love you, but don't explain anythin' to me." He glowered at Kayson.

"Ha-ha, we'd better go before he punches Quake since he knows what Quake will do—"

"Rommy," Dive barked.

She grinned. Her face didn't flame like mine.

But how come Dodge was peeved at Kayson for touching his daughter and not me?

Since I *would* be touching her.

I couldn't wait to start.

There was so much I wanted to try, and I didn't know where to begin.

A pulse of arousal tingled my pussy, dampening my panties.

Rommy turned to Kayson and me. "Ready to get out of here?"

"Yeah," Kayson said, his tone dark and rough like he was already thinking about what we were going to get up to. His cheeks tinted, and he cleared his throat while he nodded.

"Fuckin' hell," Dodge clipped.

"You're gonna have to sanitise the whole place," Dive told him.

Rommy snorted. "We'll try and keep it to the bedroom."

"Girl, go crazy," Low said as we started to walk out.

"Little bird," Dodge warned.

I was going to combust I felt that hot.

"Thanks, Mum. Later," Rommy called, and she took our hands without a care, as if she wasn't taking us to their home to get naked and have sex.

Holy crap. They all knew what we were leaving for.

I'd never be able to face them again.

CHAPTER TWENTY-FIVE

*W*hen we walked into the house, I showed them around before I took them into my bedroom. "Dad knocked the wall down between Texas's old room and mine so I could have a bigger one. And look, Eve, a window seat. Not as good as yours, but I love it."

I looked around the room, seeing what they did. It was slightly messy, but at least I'd made my bed and the sheets were practically clean.

My heart fluttered under my ribs at the reminder of getting naked with the two people I loved the most.

Turning to face them, I caught Quake's desire-filled gaze. He stood with Eve in front of him, his hands at her waist as she stared at everything she could.

Would it be rude if I moved things along?

Fuck it.

I wanted them, and they'd come here for me, so they wanted me too.

Yanking my tee up, I pulled it over my head and threw it to the floor, leaving myself in jeans and socks, since we'd taken our shoes off at the front door, and a red lacy bra.

A strangled groan dropped from Quake's lips, catching Eve's attention. She looked over at me, her eyes widening.

"Is this okay?" I asked.

Quake nodded, while Eve blushed and softly said, "Yes."

I cocked my head to the side and asked, "Nervous?"

She snorted. "The only way I'll relax is if we all rush to get naked and you get to your knees to lick me out so I can see if it's for me, which I think it will be, but the nerves are making me second-guess my choice of woman-on-woman action." Eve blanched. "I can't believe I said that."

A tingle spread between my legs.

My body hummed at the thought of being on my knees for her.

With a shrug, I offered, "I will."

Her brows dipped. "Will what?"

I flicked my gaze down her body and back up as I removed my socks and jeans. "Eat you."

Quake quietly cursed while Eve drew in a breath and shivered. "Really?"

"Babe, my mouth is watering at the thought of tasting you."

"Fuck me. Please do it," Quake pleaded.

I grinned. "Help her get undressed, Quake."

His fingers slid under her top and brushed over her

exposed skin while he waited for Eve's nod of approval. As soon as he had it, he lifted the material up and dropped it to the carpet before he made quick work of the button and zipper on her jeans. Even when he pushed them down and helped her step out of them, my gaze stayed glued on Eve's breasts hidden behind a black bra that cupped them nicely. She reached around and undid the hooks before she slowly drew it down her arms to reveal her perky breasts.

Quake stood behind Eve, his hands reaching around to cup under each one. "You want to touch them, little devil?"

I nodded.

"Do you want her to touch you, sweetheart?"

Eve whimpered. "Please."

"You heard her, Rom. Come here."

My feet ate up the carpet, and I soon stood in front of them. Quake lifted one breast, and I leaned in to kiss the top before licking down to suck a nipple into my mouth.

Eve leaned against Quake, her hands coming up to rest at my bare waist, fingers slightly digging into my skin.

"You two look stunnin' together."

Kissing across to her other breast, I told him, "It's the same with you and Eve." I licked and nipped at her nipple before straightening. "You two don't know how many times I wished I could touch you. That I wished I could kiss you, hug you, and have both of you want me like I do you two. But most of all, a fantasy of mine was picturing the two of you together. Each time I did, I'd get wet from a want so intense."

I kissed Eve, just a quick press of mouths together, and then Quake.

"My fantasy is about to come true. As a bonus, I get to play too." I did a little on-the-spot jig, which had them smiling.

"Then it's probably best we get things movin' along," Quake suggested with a gleam to his gaze.

"Oh, I concur." I looked to Eve. "You still want my mouth on your pussy?"

She shivered and nodded, cheeks heating.

"Sit on the end of the bed, babe," I told her.

Eve moved over to do as I asked, and then leaned back, hands resting on the sheets as she spread her legs.

I had the perfect view of her trimmed, glistening pussy.

My core clenched. Wetness soaked my panties.

I licked my lips before kneeling in front of her. I ducked in for the first swipe of my tongue from her hole up to her clit.

"Oh, Christ," Eve panted and nodded.

I sucked on my tongue for a moment to enjoy her taste. Humming happily, I went back for more. I gave her another long, slow swipe up and then down.

"Rommy," Eve breathed. She moaned when I ran my tongue around and over her clit, pressing down on it with quick little flicks.

"Christ, that's a sight." Quake's deep and rough voice came from behind me. I glanced over to see him half naked and his jeans undone with a hand wrapped around his cock. I couldn't wait to taste that too.

"I get to suck, lick and fuck that cock too, right?" I asked.

Quake groaned. "Yeah, little devil. This is for you and Eve."

Eve cupped my cheek, bringing my attention back to her, and she smiled. "You'll love it too. He fills you so nicely."

"Can't wait. But I have another job to excel at first." I grinned and went back to work on Eve's sweet pussy.

"Sweetheart, do you like it?" Quake asked.

Her long moan was beautiful to hear.

"Very much." Her hand cupped the back of my head, holding my mouth to her as I drank down her juices, licking and teasing everywhere. Her hole, her lips, her clit.

My stomach tingled as I pushed a finger inside her drenched, firm hole. I pulled it out and back in with another added to it.

"Oh God, Rommy." Another moan dropped from her. "That feels so good." Her body shook.

I loved that I could make Eve wiggle and pant.

"Rom, baby. God, yes."

I pumped my fingers in and out while licking, flicking, and sucking over her clit.

Her legs tightened against my head, and as she cried out, a big gush of wetness flowed down and around my fingers. I withdrew them and licked over her hole, enjoying the taste of her release.

Slowly, I kissed up her stomach and sucked a nipple into my mouth to tongue it.

My heart stuttered. My belly fluttered. I wanted her to touch me. Needed them both to have their hands on me.

Pulling back, I asked, "How are the nerves now?"

She threw her head back and laughed. My heart clenched with how gorgeous she was. When she calmed, she leaned forward to kiss me. Surprise flickered through me at her willingness to taste herself on my tongue.

Warmth hit my back, and arms circled my waist before big, strong hands glided over my stomach, hips, and breasts.

I moaned into the kiss with Eve as Quake made my body hum from where he knelt behind me.

His hand dipped, slipping under my panties. Fingers teased my entrance before one slid through my wetness and into my hole.

"Fuck," he clipped. "So wet."

Eve broke the kiss to straighten and take in what was happening. Her gaze sparked at the sight of Quake's hand in my underwear.

"She's damn drenched from eatin' you, sweetheart." His teeth scraped at my shoulder as he inserted another finger.

Moaning, I reached out, placing my hands on Eve's thighs.

"You're so beautiful, Rommy," Eve said before licking her lips. "I want to see Kayson fuck you."

My belly clenched in pleasure.

"Please," I begged.

I felt Quake's smile against my neck and saw Eve's grin before she said, "You were right. You're a lot quieter when you're busy in the bedroom."

I nodded. My mind was occupied with thinking about how wonderful everything felt.

Quake's palm rolled against my clit. A whimper escaped and then I panted out my breaths. I needed to come.

"I-I'm on the pill," I told them.

Eve pinched my chin and made me focus on her. "You want his cum inside you?"

"Yes," I breathed.

Quake groaned behind me, and I mewed in complaint when I lost his finger. His hand was in front of me, and I gaped as Eve opened her mouth and sucked down on the ones that had been inside me.

Eve moaned, closing her eyes as she ran her tongue around them, removing all my juices from his skin.

"Goddamn," I muttered, pussy clenching, heart hammering.

Quake rocked his hips into me, and I could feel his large cock against my lower back.

I wanted it.

No, I had to have it in me.

"Quake, fuck me, please."

His growl was hot. Then he ordered, "Eve, lay back. Rommy, want you naked on your knees over her."

We both moaned.

Eve scooted away to rest on her back. Quake stood and helped me up before he took the edge of my panties and pushed them down my legs. When I stepped out, I quickly climbed onto the bed, a knee at each side of Eve's hips.

A shiver raked over me when Eve's soft hands brushed over my skin. She started at my hips, up my waist, and then cupped each breast.

"Eve," I whispered, desire pumping through me.

Her smile made my breath catch. "I *want* my hands on you. I *want* to see Kayson break you apart on his cock and then for both of us to put you back together."

The bed dipped, and Quake kneeled on the mattress behind me, his hands grazing over my ass. "I like that plan, sweetheart."

"And then I'd like to taste Kayson from between your legs," Eve added softly.

Gasping, I stared down at our brave, beautiful woman.

Quake groaned low. "Fuck, I *have* to see that."

Eve went to her elbows and kissed me. I opened for her, and our tongues danced together, but she pulled away all too soon. "Flip her, Kayson. I want her between my legs and resting on me while I watch you fuck her."

A sudden laugh dropped from me when Quake made quick work of flipping me over. My lower half sat on the mattress while my upper lay over Eve between her legs.

Quake sat back and stared down at us while stroking his big, pretty cock.

"How'd I get so fuckin' lucky?"

"I hate to say it, but I got kidnapped."

They both chuckled.

"She's right. It was the only good thing that came from it," Eve said, her words almost lost beneath her breath. Her hands found me with an ease that made my pulse race, running her palms over my breasts, until her fingers caught on my nipples. The touch was sure but unhurried, teasing just enough to pull a sound from me before she moved on.

It felt like she already knew how to touch a woman. Maybe she did. Maybe she'd imagined this before, the way I had. Whatever it was, she wasn't shy about it. The confidence in her touch—steady and certain—lit something in me that Quake never could. His power was raw, consuming to me. Hers was quiet and patient, like she was discovering something wondrous.

Quake kissed my stomach. "Now, we get to keep her." He dipped again to lick over my skin.

I nodded and hummed. "Yes. Keep me. Do anything you want to me. But just get inside me."

They laughed again.

But thankfully Quake listened.

One hand went to the bed and the other he used to guide his cock. The tip brushed against my soaked hole, and another whimper escaped.

Slowly, he pushed his big prick in, filling me deliciously and slowly. I'd never had a dick this size, and the way I snugly surrounded him had my body lighting with new hunger. I couldn't wait to be fucked by him. He dropped the other hand to the bed and watched between us as he fitted all the way in.

I smiled up at him. "Your cock feels incredible."

Eve laughed lightly. "Doesn't it?"

I clenched my walls around him, and he cursed as I all but begged, "Move, please."

"I ain't gonna last after watchin' you two."

"That's okay. I just need you to move."

"Wait one more second—"

"Fuck me, Daddy," I tried.

Quake groaned and pulled his cock from me before thrusting in hard.

"Yes," I cried.

"That's it, Kayson," Eve encouraged. "Bring out all her noises. Punish her pussy."

He did.

His hips slapped against mine as he drilled in and out of me while Eve pinched, tugged, and played with my skin.

My body vibrated with the pleasure they showered me with, pulling new sounds from me that I didn't know I could make, but I loved that they were drawing them forward.

"Shit. Fuck. You feel good." Quake groaned and slid a hand under my ass, gripping my cheek while holding me in place for his hard thrusts.

"You're going to fill her with your cum, Kayson. Give her every last drop and then I'm going to eat it out of her. Make sure Rommy knows she belongs to us. That she's ours."

This was perfect.

This was us.

The way we touched, played, and fucked was a high I'd continuously want. Their scents mixing, even their sweat and the feel of their skin was addicting.

"Fuckin' hell," Quake chanted.

I panted and moaned and whimpered through it all.

"Yes. God, yes, Quake," I cried when my orgasm hit, and I squeezed around him as he still fucked me hard and fast.

"Christ," he clipped, hips stuttering before he groaned loudly as he pumped his cum into me.

I shuddered when he slipped free from me and smiled like a content cat.

"Help her sit for a second," Eve said.

Quake pulled my upper body forward by both arms, enough for Eve to slip out from under me. He rolled to my side, mouth slanting over mine, kissing me sweetly and softly.

My legs were pushed apart, and we broke the kiss to watch Eve lie on her stomach and lower her mouth to my pussy.

"You might need to fuck me after this," Eve said. "Watching you two has my pussy pulsing."

Quake grinned. "Don't worry, sweetheart. No doubt after watching you make our girl come, I'll be ready for another round."

Could a person die of too many orgasms?

I may soon find out.

Yippee.

CHAPTER TWENTY-SIX

QUAKE

Since Rommy had time off, and we'd finally come up for air two days later, the first thing she wanted to show us was Ballarat and the family she had there. When she parked out front of a tattoo shop and climbed out, I undid my seat belt and realised I wasn't fast enough. In the next second, Rommy was at my door, opening mine and Eve's in the back.

"Come on, come on. Texas might have a client, but you can meet Hex and Mon." She gasped, taking our hands and dragging us towards the front door. "Maya and Swan might even be here. You'll love Swan. She's such a sweet, shy woman. She's dating Drake. His club name is Dragon, and he's Talon's youngest boy. Eve, he's a twin, too, with his sister, Ruby."

Eve smiled. "I haven't actually met another twin sibling before."

Rommy nodded. "You will. There's also Josie, Pick, and Billy's kids, Payton and Theodore. And Killer and Ivy have twins too." She dropped our hands and turned to face us, beaming before she wrapped her arms around our waists, hugging us tightly. "I can do this. And I can do this...." She went to her toes and puckered her lips at me. Grinning, I bent and kissed her before she did the same to Eve.

Sliding my hand around Eve's waist, above Rommy's arm, I reached out to cup the back of Rommy's head. "You can do anythin' you want."

She cackled. "Oh, pooky, don't say that to me. You don't know where my mind can go."

Smirking, I said, "Bring it on."

Eve laughed. "You know, I'm down for tying Kayson up so we can both torture him."

A thrill ran down my spine. "Hell, I like the sound of that."

Rommy hummed, leaning into us. "I'm already picturing the things Eve and I can do."

The door behind us opened. "Huh, guess Dodge wasn't lying," Texas said. "Instead of gropin' each other at my entrance, how about you lot come in?"

Rommy spun and launched herself at her brother, who caught her and hugged her tightly.

"Bro, Eve and Quake are here, and they're *mine*."

I moved my arm up to around Eve's shoulders as we watched Rommy with humour.

This was right.

It felt good.

She was meant to be with us.

And Christ, I couldn't stop feeling like my body was full to the goddamn brim with happiness.

Two women to love and who will love me back.

"Heard they took you on," Texas teased. "I've got Easton and Lan in the room. Easton's gettin' more ink."

Rommy gasped and shoved her brother out of the way as she ran down the hall.

Texas snorted. "Come on in."

When we stepped through, a woman behind the counter whistled. "You're a fucking giant. No wonder you need two women to worship that big body."

"Fuckin' hell, Mon," Texas clipped before calling louder, "Hex, Mon's droolin' again."

A heavily inked guy stepped out of a door close by to stare at us. "Huh, fair." Then he disappeared again.

Mon cocked a brow at Texas.

He groaned and palmed his face. "Welcome to the mad world." He faced us and crossed his arms over his chest.

I knew what was coming. I was expecting it.

"My sister is a shining light in what can be a dark world. She's to be cherished. She ain't second best. She's top-tier."

Eve nodded. "We couldn't agree more, which is why we were sure about our feelings before coming here."

I nodded. "We wouldn't have travelled halfway around the world for someone who doesn't mean everythin' to us," I told him.

Texas eyed us for a beat longer, until a certain devil stuck her head out a door and yelled, "Stop messing with them, bro. Guys, get your cute butts in here."

Chuckling, Eve and I followed Texas down the hallway and into a tidy and spacious room. Another guy covered in ink sat on the table while Rommy rested on the armrest of the couch beside another older guy. Rommy thumbed at him, saying, "This is Lan. On the table is Easton. Lan is a part-time detective and a private investigator too. Easton is a paramedic."

"Hi," Easton said with a wave.

"Hey. Eve and Quake, right?" Lan asked.

I nodded. "Yeah, man."

"We're dating Rommy," Eve supplied before her cheeks heated.

"Aww," Rommy cooed, then skipped over to hug Eve to her. "They're stuck with me as theirs now." She kissed Eve quickly and moved over to the table. "Come have a look at what my brother's doing."

Texas had just sat down with fresh gloves on, but he pushed his chair back to make room for us.

"That'd have to hurt. Looks great, but the pain, man," I said when I saw the lion on his shin.

Easton chuckled. "I'm used to the pain now."

Guessed that was true since every inch of him was practically covered.

"Better get back to it," Texas said, so Eve and I moved over to the couch. I sat and pulled Eve down on my lap while we talked with Lan. Easton and Texas added in what they wanted to say every now and then too.

After a while, Easton hissed. "Damn that highlighting."

Texas snorted. "You should know by now it's the worst part."

Easton groaned. "I do, but let me complain."

Lan chuckled. "You wanna tap out, East?"

Easton glared back at him. "No."

"Just about done," Texas told him before the gun started buzzing again. "You guys staying in town for a bit?" Texas asked, flicking his gaze up.

Rommy nodded. "I want to for a few days. Got to visit Channa's, the compound, and Ballarat Wildlife Park."

"I'm sure Talon will offer some rooms at the compound," Texas said.

"Rooms? We only need one room, bro."

"La-la-la, my sister doesn't do any of that stuff."

We all chuckled.

"We'll drop into the compound to visit anyway and see what Talon says," Rommy suggested.

Texas shook his head. "He ain't around today. But Griz will probably be there. He'll let you know. I doubt it'll be a problem."

"Cool, cool. I'll let you know when we find out so we can do dinner one night or something."

"Sounds good, Rom." He glanced to me and Eve. "How long you two in town for?"

Shit.

We hadn't even talked about what the plan was.

"We're not sure yet," Eve said.

There was a tap at the door before it was pushed open, and a guy with shoulder-length hair stepped in. He tipped his chin our way as he approached Easton.

"Hey, how's it goin'?" He dipped and kissed Easton on the lips.

Eve and I swung our gazes to Lan, who smiled while watching the men.

"Highlighting" was all Easton said.

The guy grinned. "You've got this."

Easton waved him away

"Parker," Rommy called.

He straightened and grinned at her. "Kid, what's happenin'?"

He walked our way as Rommy announced, "Same old. Except, this is Eve and Quake and they're mine."

His grin grew. "Yours, hey?"

She nodded. "Yep. All mine."

He held his hand out to me, and I shook it. "Where are you two from?" he asked after shaking Eve's hand.

Only we didn't answer because he leaned down and kissed Lan too.

Hell, it was no wonder Rommy was comfortable to explore this with us. She'd grown up around more than two people in a relationship. I remembered her mentioning a Josie, Pick, and Billy, but never heard about Easton, Lan, and Parker.

"We're from Searchlight, Nevada."

He eyed my cut. "A club?"

"Yeah, the Diamond MC."

"The ones who helped rescue me," Rommy said.

"They're also the club we helped when we took custody of Harred Plank as soon as he stepped off the plane," Lan supplied.

"Hell, no wonder your names were familiar," I said. "Thanks for assistin' the club."

Parker shrugged. "Always willin' to help out. But especially for the Hawks brothers."

The tattoo gun's buzzing stopped as Texas said, "All done."

Easton sighed. "Thank God."

Lan and Parker shared a look with a grin before they went over to their third. Rommy moved onto the couch and squished herself against us. Smiling, I curled an arm around her shoulders, and Eve took her hand to hold on her lap while we watched Lan and Parker admire Easton's new piece.

When Texas's phone rang, he glanced at the screen and called, "Rom, grab that. It's Maya."

She jumped up to answer it. "Girl, where the heck are you? I thought you'd be here at my brother's. Guess what, I have Eve and Quake here with me. They came all the way to Australia to claim me." She beamed over at us and blew us a kiss. "I should have known you already knew since my brother's the biggest gossiper out there."

"Fuck off. That'd be you," Texas complained before he went back to talking to the others.

Rommy nodded at something Maya said. "Right, got it. Zara and Talon's dinner tomorrow night. Will you and bro be there? ... Aww, date night. That's cute." Texas shot her a glare. "Maya, Texas is glaring at me. ... She said not to be mean." He rolled his eyes. "Are you sure he said it was okay we can stay at the compound? ... Okay, thanks, and tell them thanks and we'll see them tomorrow night. Love you, bye." She turned to us. "Dad already talked to Talon, so he knows we're in town, and we have a room at the compound. Yay! You'll both get to meet more people." She skipped back over to sit next to us. "Plus, we've been invited to dinner. Mum and Dad will come down for it too."

I didn't tell her we'd already gathered everything from her one-sided conversation. Instead, I said, "Sounds great, little devil." I kissed her forehead, but she tipped her head back, and I gave her what she wanted by slanting my lips over hers.

"Little devil? That's a perfect name for my sister," Texas said with a chuckle.

"I like it," Rommy said.

"Before you go back to Caroline Springs, you'll have to come to our place for dinner," Easton offered.

Rommy gasped. "We'd love to. Easton has so many dogs. Not that we'd be coming just to see them. You know I love hanging out with you. I used to go to their house when I was younger. And Dive and Mena's... I stayed there a lot. But I also loved going to Beast and Knife's as well."

"Sounds like you had a lot of people you could rely on," Eve said.

"Exactly." Rommy nodded.

We said goodbye to Easton, Lan, and Parker. While Texas walked them out, I brushed a hand over Rommy's hair as Eve moved off my lap to sit on Rommy's other side.

"I'm glad you have so much love and care surroundin' you, Rommy," I told her.

"It's helped me learn to be who I wanted to be."

"I think it's amazing," Eve said, leaning into her. "Kayson had a great upbringing too."

Snorting, I shrugged. "I wouldn't say it was great."

Eve started laughing.

"What?" Rommy asked, looking from me to her.

"My parents are hippies."

"What's wrong with that?" Rommy asked.

"Nothing," Eve said. "They love their sweet little boy so very much."

"Aww, that sounds cute."

I sighed. "They're also nudists." Rommy's gaze widened, and she slapped her hand over her mouth. "When they drop in to the club, the brothers think it's hilarious to get them drunk and high, which they do a lot in their community, but they always decide it's a good idea to strip and walk around in front of everyone."

Rommy couldn't hide her laughter. It slipped through her fingers.

"They tried to get Kayson to join them. He went beet red and hid in his room. They're a really cute couple."

"Who'd rather be at one with the land and live out in no-man's land with a bunch of other old people where a hospital is forever away. It's dangerous."

Rommy wrapped her arms around one of mine. "You worry. It's cute. Is there anyone there with a medical background?"

"I wouldn't know. I love my parents, but I can't go and visit them when they're all walkin' around naked. That shit just ain't right."

"I want to meet them," Rommy said.

Shit.

"I'd love to go visit them, too, Kayson," Eve added.

Double fucking shit.

I'd give these two the world.

And they already knew it.

Pinching the bridge of my nose, I sighed. "Fine. One year we'll go see them, but you two will have to lead me around because I'll be blindfolded."

"I don't want to know your kinks," Texas said as he entered the room again.

The women laughed while I dropped my head back, heat hitting my cheeks. Yet, my smile remained as I was here with Eve and Rommy, and they were both mine.

CHAPTER TWENTY-SEVEN

I knocked on the door, then looked over my shoulder to wink and blow a kiss to my people. Eve moved up behind me to place her hands to my hips and playfully nip at my neck.

"You know," I said, "I never thought you'd want to kiss me let alone"—the door opened—"go down on me," I finished.

Eve paled and took a step back while Quake moved in behind her to steady her.

"Talon," I cried before hugging the man.

"Christ, kid. I could have done without knowin' what goes on in the bedroom."

"Well, we ain't playing with LEGO." While Quake choked on his laugh, I took a step their way, waving my hands up and down our bodies. "Talon, this is Eve and

258

Quake. Guys, this is Talon, the big boss man of the Hawks MC."

"Talon, it's good to meet you," Quake said, holding out his hand.

Talon stepped forward and gripped his palm, shaking it.

"Hi," Eve offered.

He tipped his chin up at her. "So, you two decided on datin' Rommy."

Quake nodded. "Yes, sir."

"Better do fuckin' right by her," he warned.

"Awww, that's so sweet," I cooed, making Talon sigh.

"Honey, who is it?" Zara appeared in the doorway and gasped. "You're here." She glared at Talon. "You didn't scare or threaten them, right?"

"Never, kitten." Talon smirked as he leaned in to kiss Zara's temple before disappearing into the house.

Zara stepped back and waved us in. "Come in, come in."

I skipped through and gave her a big hug. "Zara, this is Quake and Eve."

Zara smiled widely as she closed the door. "Low's told me so much about you two, it's like I already know you."

"All good we hope," Eve said, with a shy, nervous smile.

Zara laughed. "It is. And she didn't exaggerate." Zara looked up at Quake. "You're a big guy."

Quake grinned. "Thanks."

"Ma—Jesus Christ, were you born from giants?" Dragon said when he stepped into the living room.

"Drake," Zara snapped.

I cackled. "You should see Blaze. He's a bit bigger."

"No, thanks. I don't want to look mini compared to them."

"I like the way you are," Swan said, walking in.

"Birdy." He hooked an arm around Swan's neck and kissed her cheek. He was so much like his father. When he looked back, he asked, "Are you two sure you're ready to put up with Rommy?"

Zara sighed at her son while Swan hit his stomach and Dragon just grinned.

I glanced back and saw Eve had thinned her lips, and the smile slipped from Quake's.

"Rommy ain't someone who needs to be put up with, so don't fuckin' say that shit," Quake warned before he moved his attention to Zara. "Sorry for the language."

Zara waved him off as she gave him another pleased smile. "It's fine."

Eve's hands pressed to her stomach. "We understand you're all close, but teasing in that way, where it questions Rommy's importance, really puts us on edge."

Quake grunted.

Goddamn, they had to stop being adorable.

Happy tears welled, and I cried, "You guys." I moved into them and was wrapped up tightly in their arms.

"Yeah, you two will be good for her," I heard Dragon say. "Name's Dragon, and this is my old lady, Swan."

"Quake and Eve," Quake replied over my head, which I had smooched up against their arms.

"What's taking so long? I need to eat." I turned to see Channa with Coyote at her back.

"You don't want to mess with her when she's hungry now," Coyote warned.

Channa didn't respond as she was too busy gaping up at Quake.

Coyote grumbled under his breath and covered her eyes.

Laughing, I rushed over to hug them both. "Coyote and Channa, these are my Eve and Quake."

Channa pulled Coyote's hand down. "Hi. It's so nice to meet you both."

"You too. Rommy's always tellin' us about how good your bakery is," Quake said.

Eve nodded. "We're dropping in tomorrow. But between these two, you might need to restock the shelves a couple of times."

I laughed, winking at them. "It's true. Quake loves food as much as me."

"It'll be a pleasure to see you all there."

"Now let's head back so Channa can eat," Coyote said.

We walked down the hallway that led to the kitchen and dining area where Mum and Dad already sat at the table with Talon.

I rushed up to hug them both. "How was the ride?"

"Cold," Mum answered.

Dad snorted. "Wasn't that bad."

Mum scoffed. "The temp always drops when travelling this way." Mum glanced up at Eve and Quake. "Hey, you two. How are you liking Ballarat?"

Eve leaned in and mock whispered, "I think it's cold too."

"Damn right, girl. See, I'm not the only one." Mum waved a hand to the large table. "Come, take a seat."

Before they could move, a door banged open before we heard, "I am here. Bow down at my greatness."

"I'm gonna kill him if he dinted our goddamn wall," Talon bit out.

"Honey," Zara said.

When Julian and Mattie entered, I swooped in for a hug, wrapping them both in an arm. "Hey, hi, hello."

"Oh, sweetums, it's so good to see you. Our visit after you got back wasn't long enough." He cupped my cheek and kissed my forehead.

"Rommy, it's great to see you." Mattie smiled. "And before you ask, Aelia has a cold, so she couldn't make it. But she wants to see you soon to talk about some book series she's found."

Perking up, I nodded. "I'll text her. But come here." I took their hands and walked them over to Eve and Quake.

Julian noticed Quake first. "Sweet Mother Mary, you're even better in person." He then glanced at Eve. "You both are."

"They're mine," I told him.

Quake and Eve grinned.

Julian's brows pinched. "As in your friends, right, pumpkin?"

I guessed news hadn't travelled to everyone.

Gaping, I asked, "You haven't heard?"

Julian shook his head. "I know I love a good gossip, but I've been busy this month."

"They're mine," I told him.

He patted me on the top of the head. "You said that."

"You're dating them?" Mattie guessed.

I grinned and bounced on my feet. "Yep."

Julian gaped. "You lucky little mortal."

He turned to Mattie and went to open his mouth, but Mattie quickly said, "No. You know I don't share."

Julian gave him a sultry smirk as he wrapped his hands

around Mattie's upper arm and leaned into him. "This is true. Plus, I'd claw anyone's eyes out if they touched you."

"Great. That's sorted. Let's fuckin' eat," Talon ordered from his seat at the head of the table. He leaned forward and uncovered the trays of barbequed meat and vegetables in front of him before throwing the lids to the floor behind him. "Drake, grab the other two lids for me," he ordered since Drake was closer to them.

"Talon," Zara snapped, slapping at her husband's arm.

"Relax, kitten, I'll pick them up later."

Zara rolled her eyes.

"Grab a chair," Low offered.

"Julian and Mattie," Zara called, pointing down to the opposite end of the table. "You guys are sharing that end together because Ruby and Dillon are still joining us, and they'll sit by Drake."

"We don't mind being squished together at all," Julian told her.

With Talon at the head of the twelve-seater table, well, thirteen with an extra chair at the other end, Dad sat on his left with Zara on Talon's right. Beside her was Swan and then Drake, with the two extra seats spare. So, since Mum was next to Dad, I moved Eve over to sit by her, then Quake, and I took my seat on the end near Julian.

It was crowded but felt good because it was all family.

As we dished up our meals, Ruby shouted from the front of the house, "We're here."

Zara smiled, and we all looked to the entryway where Ruby walked in, followed by Dillon.

"Hey, Dilbert," Dragon called.

"Shut up, Drake," Ruby snapped.

I gasped and looked around Quake to Eve. "I forgot I told you Dragon and Ruby are twins too."

Eve smiled softly before she looked to Ruby. "Hi, I'm Eve. I have a twin back in America. A brother too. His name's Tech."

I was about to explain who Eve and Quake were to me, but before I could say anything, Quake did. "Hey, I'm Quake. Eve and I are datin' Rommy."

My grin was super big when I saw their gazes widen. Ruby looked to me, and I nodded. "Yep, I snagged two. They came to Australia to tell me they love *me*. Me! Can you believe it?"

Quake curled an arm around my shoulders and kissed my temple. "It's easy to believe because the love is for you, Rommy."

"Exactly," Eve added.

Julian sniffed, and I caught Dad and Talon sharing a look. They both tipped their chins up at each other, and I knew without a doubt they'd accepted *my* people.

Ruby cleared her throat. "Congratulations, Rommy." She turned to Eve and Quake as she and Dillon sat down. "As you heard, I'm Ruby, and this is my boyfriend, Dillon."

"I thought it was Dilbert," Quake said.

Dragon, Dad, and Talon chuckled. Even Dillon smiled, but Ruby lifted her hand and smacked her twin in the back of the head. "See what you're doing." She sighed.

"It's fine, baby," Dillon said.

"At least he's a good sport about it," I said. "I'm sure Dragon and Talon call you different names because it's their way to show they care about you," I suggested and waited five seconds before—

"What the fuck, Rommy. No, I don't," Dragon grumbled.

"You've lost it, kid," Talon clipped.

Swan and Zara hid their smiles behind their hands.

Dillon sat up straighter as Ruby said, "That's actually sweet."

Dragon picked up his knife and pointed it at me. "I'm gonna kill you."

I snorted. "I'd like to see you try."

But it was Eve that surprised me by saying, "You won't even get near her."

"Damn right," Quake added, glaring at Dragon.

Gushy, mushy feelings filled me, and while I cooed, hugging Quake's arm, I reached over for Eve's hand. I finally had people, who weren't my friends and family, at my back.

People who I love, and they love me.

Life couldn't get better.

Except, they'll go home one day.

My smile slipped, but I busied myself by grabbing more food as the others talked around me, asking Eve and Quake questions.

What would I do when they left for America?

And they would leave. They had to. Quake had businesses.

So, what was I going to do? I glanced at all the people at the table. Could I leave them?

Shaking my head, I stuffed some meat, not Quake's, in my mouth and pushed those thoughts back for now. I just wanted to enjoy the night and not get lost in other things.

One day soon, we would sort it out.

CHAPTER TWENTY-EIGHT

QUAKE

A long groan of pleasure rolled out of me. I looked down at the minxes who were kneeling on Rommy's bed, one at each side, while leaning over to lick and suck my cock.

"One of you sit on my face," I ordered, relieved as hell we were back in Caroline Springs.

They shared a glance before smiling at each other. Rommy climbed up to straddle my head, facing Eve. My little red-haired tease went back to sucking me off.

"Christ," I clipped, then shoved my face up to do my own teasing against Rommy's pussy. I gripped her hips to hold her in place and enjoyed each whimpered sound as I tongued and mouthed her hole and clit.

"Quake, oh God." Her hands swept up and down over my chest and stomach while Eve bobbed over my cock, her mouth wet, warm, the suction around my dick like a tight snatch.

No way would I last.

They'd been teasing me for nearly an hour already.

And I fucking loved it.

I loved them.

We fit together like we'd been made for each other.

"Just there, yes. Yes, Quake," Rommy cried, rolling her pussy back and forth over my tongue and mouth. I kept flicking and licking and drinking her juices like a thirsty man.

They made me thirsty.

Watching them was the best fucking show on the planet.

Another groan rolled out of me. I was damn close.

I needed our little devil to finish first.

I toyed with my tongue over her clit. She gasped, tensed, and then a flood of her cum wet my face. I ate at her, licking and sucking and teasing until she slapped at my stomach. As soon as I released her legs, she climbed off and slid down the bed to kiss me.

Groaning into her mouth, I emptied my cum into Eve's, which she eagerly drank down.

When Rommy pulled back, both of us were breathing heavily.

She grinned, which I returned before looking down my body to Eve who rested her chin to my hip while watching Rommy and me.

"Your turn, sweetheart."

She smiled and shook her head.

Brows pinched, I asked, "Why not?"

"I had busy fingers while I watched you two."

Fucking loved that we all got hot from watching each other.

I held out my arm that Rommy wasn't resting her head on while she traced a finger over my chest and told Eve, "Then get up here."

She quickly crawled up the bed and slumped down at my side, her hand finding Rommy's on my chest and holding it.

"Are we sleeping or watching a movie?" Eve asked.

"I'm happy to do either," I said. "Rommy?" She was being strangely quiet again. It'd happened a few times over the last week.

Usually, she bounced back and rambled about something after coming, but her continued silence was suspicious.

"Maybe a movie?" she said.

She liked to pick if we offered her choices. Why didn't she now?

Eve and I shared a look, both of us puzzled.

Kissing Eve's forehead and then Rommy's, I gently slapped their asses. "Let's get into comfortable clothes, have snacks, and watch somethin'." We still had Rommy's parents' place to ourselves, which gave us the freedom to do what we wanted and talk freely. If Rommy didn't snap out of her thoughts soon, Eve and I'd have to figure out what was on her mind.

Obviously, it was something big, and I worried it was about our future. Something we'd been putting off since no one wanted to be a downer on our time here. But I was sure we also put the talk off because we were scared that nothing would get sorted out.

LATER, my gut was a mess since Rommy was still quiet and hadn't eaten anything. Now, she just rested over us on the couch without rambling about what we were watching or whatever else she was thinking.

This shit was serious.

Eve and I shared another look. She nodded down at Rommy, but I shook my head and tipped my chin up at her.

Rommy suddenly sighed. "You guys have been here two weeks. I think it's time we have *the* talk."

With my arm around Eve's shoulders, I felt her tense as I did.

"What do you mean, Rom?" Eve asked, brushing her fingers up and down Rommy's arm.

She rolled to her back, so her head and upper torso were on my lap and her waist and butt rested on Eve's legs.

She bit her bottom lip, and a flash of concern punched me in the gut.

"We haven't really brought it up, and I understand it's a big decision. I'm sure no one wants to put pressure on anyone when it comes to picking a place to settle our lives in, which is why I want to take that pressure away by saying I'm coming back with you both to America."

Holy fuck.

Did she just—

"I mean, I've looked it up. I can move. I just need the right visa for it. There's an employment-based type." She suddenly sat and moved to the end of the couch facing us. "Do you think the club would hire me to be their mechanic and sponsor me? I know you guys take your rides to one close by, but I'm good at what I do. If I get a work visa, that means I could stay."

"Rommy," Eve whispered.

She cocked her head to the side. "Unless you want to do long distance?"

"No," I clipped. "We want you twenty-four-fuckin'-seven. This is a commitment. The weeks we've been here have shown us how good this relationship is."

Eve reached out and took her hand as tears welled in Rommy's gaze. "Kayson's right. We just got you. We're not losing you to a different continent. But we want you to be completely sure. This is a big choice, Rommy."

"We could alternate. A year here and year there," I suggested.

Eve nodded. "Yes. I like that. It would work for your families."

Rommy sniffed, wiped at her eyes, and then shook her head. "No. I love you both for thinking that, but we can't waste money on travelling each year. We're going to make this work in America. Yeah, I'll miss my family like crazy, but there's many ways I'll still hear from them and see them." She pushed her shoulders back and told us, "I'm moving to America. I want to be there to join your world and make it ours."

My chest expanded, and hope filled it.

But worry kicked me in the gut.

She'd be leaving here. Her family.

Eve gripped her top near her throat. "Rommy, are you sure? Your family...."

"Is here in Australia. They always will be here, but what we've got going means we're family, too, right? I'll miss my family, but I won't ever be lonely or feel unloved because I have both of you, and you two mean everything to me."

Reaching over, I picked her up, spun her around, and planted her ass on my lap. Eve snuggled in close too, touching both of us.

"Rom, you're everythin' to us," I told her. "We'd love to have you in America with us."

Eve nodded. "We can sort out the visa, and if we can't get you the right one, I'm sure we can get Blaze to work something out. We'll figure it all out, but knowing we're not going home without you eases me so much."

I grunted. "Fuck yeah it does. I hated the thought of leavin' without you."

Rommy hugged us both before sitting back. "I'll have to come back to meet my brother's baby. And I'm sure they'll visit me in the States, but we'll make it all work. I just can't do without you two."

Tears filled Eve's gaze. "And we can't do without you."

Leaning down, I kissed Rommy's neck. "Like you said, we're stuck together now." I nudged my nose against her chin. "Been meanin' to say, you're mine as much as Eve is, and I'd love it if you called me Kayson too."

Her smile was bright and warm. She cupped the side of my neck. "I'd love that, and I will, at times. But I like Quake too."

Grinning, I squeezed her ass. "Call me whatever you want, whenever you want."

"Deal," she said before she kissed me.

A phone chimed, and I felt Eve move to check. "Rommy, it's for you."

She leaned against my chest as she took her phone from Eve. "It's my Mum. They're close by and want to make sure we're all dressed so they can stop by to grab some things."

Laughing, I suggested, "Maybe we should close your bedroom door."

"I'll get it," Eve said.

"I'm going to tell them," Rommy said softly.

"About comin' to America?"

"Yeah. I don't want to put it off. We need to get sorted as soon as possible to start our lives together in the US."

"How do you think they'll take it?"

She hummed while thinking. "There'll be a lot of glaring from Dad and worry from Mum. Dad might want to punch you for stealing me."

Grinning, I wrapped my arms around her. "I'll take anythin' on if it means we *can* steal you. Now let's quickly tidy a little before they arrive." I helped her up, and we went to work straightening things.

I had to make a better impression since we were taking their only daughter to the other side of the world.

Fuck.

If it was me and my daughter, I'd hate her lovers for taking her.

By the time we heard a bike roll in, the place looked decent, and I was ready for the hate, because no matter what, we weren't going home without Rommy.

We were sitting on the couch again, with Rommy in the middle, when the front door opened and Low peeked in.

"They're dressed," she said behind her before entering.

"Didn't I text you back?" Rommy asked, reaching for her phone on the coffee table.

"No, but I saw you'd read it, so I presumed you'd be busy getting into clothes."

Rommy stood and clasped her hands in front of her as her dad walked in.

Dodge looked at his daughter and clipped, "Fuck."

"What? What is it?" Low asked, looking from each person before settling on Rommy. "Oh." Tears brimmed in Low's eyes, and her bottom lip trembled.

Dodge ground his teeth together.

"Mum, Dad. I love being here with my family, but I belong with Eve and Kayson in America." Eve and I stood behind her, a supporting hand on each shoulder.

Low turned her head away, but I didn't miss the tears falling. She nodded and faced her daughter again, letting out a rough, unamused laugh. "I tried preparing myself for this." Her lips thinned, and she sniffed, shaking her head. "But it's going to hurt seeing you go, no matter what, and yet, we still understand, girl."

"Mum," Rommy whimpered.

"You always have a home here, no matter what," Low told her before she turned away, looking to her man. "Trey."

His jaw clenched again. "I get you gotta follow your heart, kid." There was another clench. "Won't be the same without you."

"Dad."

He cleared his throat and sniffed. "Yeah. Got shit to grab." He started to stomp off but turned back and glowered our way. "Fuckin' take care of her like the precious treasure she is."

"We will," Eve said quickly.

"Always," I told him.

He grunted and swept out his arm. Rommy ran, slamming herself against her father's chest. We heard her sob as she clutched at him. Tears welled, and he dropped his head back, blinking up at the ceiling, grinding his teeth together.

Eve moved over to Low and wrapped an arm around her waist. Low gave her a watery smile.

Dodge took a shuddering breath and locked his emotions down before he ducked down and kissed the top of her hair. "Come on, now. You ain't leavin' this second. We still got a couple of days together. But, kid, I want you to know you enriched my life the day I came to pick you and your brother up. And since then, I've enjoyed each and every day we've had together. Just because you'll be oceans away doesn't mean we won't have more time together. Fuckin' love you worldwide, kid."

"Love you too," she cried.

I'd make sure to find a way for them to see each other often. Both of my women deserved the goddamn best in life, and I'd make sure they found it each and every day. Even if we hit rough spots, we'd come out better in the end because I wouldn't fucking lose them.

EPILOGUE

ROMANIA

"Rommy, get your ass back here," Quake demanded as I rolled away and climbed out of bed to stand beside it. His cum dripped out of me, but I couldn't climax anymore. We'd already been at it for hours.

Pointing at my legs, I told them, "Look, they're wobbly. You two have drained me dry."

Eve giggled and then pouted. "But I wanted to eat Kayson's cum out of you."

My belly quivered, and I groaned. It was her favourite thing to do, and usually, I'd love that. But I really did feel drained in the best possible way. Plus, I had things I needed to do. "If I didn't have to get downstairs to work and we hadn't already made each other come twice, I would have your head between my legs in seconds. You're going to have to settle for licking our cum off Quake's cock." I smiled and blew them a kiss before rushing towards the bathroom for a shower.

By the time I was done, they were a panting mess tangled together on the bed.

I skipped over to them and gave them a quick kiss. "See you later. Love you both."

Quake winked. "Love you, little devil."

"Love you, Rom."

Nearing the door, Quake called, "Hey, don't forget we're going for a ride later."

"Yep, I remember." I opened the door and stepped out, turning back to peek in and tell them, "I put it in my phone, so it'll remind me to stop working."

"Good."

"Later, my gorgeous people."

"Bye," Eve called.

"Later, little devil."

Once I got downstairs, I headed straight for the kitchen after greeting the people mingling around. I pushed through the double doors. "Hey, hi, hello," I called.

"Morning, Rommy," Dusty called from the counter.

"Rom," Country said from where he stood next to his wife.

"Hey, Rommy. We got that part in for Loyal's bike," Saint told me before he took a sip of his coffee. I headed for the food and grabbed a muffin.

"You're going to turn into a muffin one day," Gun teased.

"That's okay. Then Eve and Quake can eat—"

"Nope," Country quickly said.

The doors opened behind us to let in Henri and Blaze. "Bonjour."

Everyone greeted them, though all we got from Blaze was a grunt. The guy was such a hoot. I sidled up beside him, and he stared down at me.

Smiling, I opened my mouth, but he cut me off when he said, "Not happening."

"Just one little rumble to see who would win?"

"No."

"I'll get you to give in one day," I told him with a huff and took another bite.

"Chéri, will you be coming to opening night in a couple of days?" Henri asked me. "Since we are past the delays now," he muttered, more to himself than me.

Secretly I was glad there were a couple of things that stopped them from opening because now I would be here for it.

"Of course, I wouldn't miss it. Quake said he'll be working the bar, so Eve and I want to be there for him too."

"That is sweet. Our boy, Sawyer, will be stripping on that night too."

Blaze grumbled under his breath.

Henri shot him a look. "Mon amour, we have spoken about this. We need to let our butterfly soar and find his own way when it comes to making his money. All we can do is support him." Henri grinned. "Besides, I am sure Loyal will keep a close eye on him."

"I thought he was at Polished that night," Country commented.

"He has asked for a shift change from Wreck."

Oh man, I so wanted to be there to see Loyal watching Sawyer dance. It was gonna be epic.

Another plus was that Eve and I would get to admire Quake in his tight shirt as he worked the bar.

"Question," I called. "Are people allowed to hit other people if they try and hit on their people?"

"Should I worry that I understood what she said?" Saint asked.

Gun snorted. "We all got it. Rommy, you can't attack anyone if they ask for Quake's number."

"But—"

"Or if they brush his hand," Saint said, like he'd read my mind already.

"But—"

"Or if they come near his body," Country added quickly. "Just don't hurt anyone without permission from one of the owners."

I grinned. "Sounds like a plan."

"Should we worry about that smile?" Dusty asked.

"Oui, we should. Do you forget that my Blaze is one of the owners and he would give her permission for a small incident?"

We all looked at a grinning Blaze. I cackled like a madwoman.

Country sighed. "Permission from anyone but Blaze, Rommy."

I shot him a finger gun. "You got it, boss man." I took another bite of the muffin as I walked over to grab a strawberry milk out. Dusty was so kind when she stocked up after she found out it was what I liked to drink in the mornings.

I loved being here. It really was like home, and they were fast becoming my family.

However, no one would top Eve or Quake.

They were my everything.

I still mostly called Quake his club name. I used Kayson, plus Daddy, for the bedroom. But I thought it cute that Eve used it a lot more than me. Like they were the OGs, but they accepted me, and now I was allowed to do things with them.

And we did *many* things.

A couple of the brothers had asked for us to keep it down or to let them watch.

It was a no to both requests.

I'd stab a guy in the eye if anyone saw Eve's and Quake's sex faces. I was a bit more feral when it came to protecting those two.

Just the other day I saw a guy shoving Quake. I didn't know who it was since they were facing away, so I charged, launched, and put him in a chokehold. Quake had to pull me off Snake's back. But it was his fault for not wearing his cut. If I'd known it was one of the brothers, I wouldn't have attacked.

Well, not as aggressively as I had. Maybe a little light pushing.

Once I had my drink, I called, "Got to get to work. See you all later."

Everyone called something out as I left, except Blaze of course, and I made my way outside to the garage the club was doing up for me to work out of. There was still some painting and shelving to do, but I had my little bay I worked from, which was out of the other brothers' way while they finished. No one was there yet, though. I took the last bite of the muffin. After swallowing, I gulped the milk down to wash it all away before I grabbed my headphones, connected my music, and put on the coveralls. Placing the headphones on, I got to work on Loyal's ride, noticing the part Saint had been talking about in the box on the counter. I didn't need it just yet. I still had a few things to do before then.

I worked for a while, only pausing when my phone vibrated. I tugged it free and saw a FaceTime from Mum.

I answered, "Hey, hi, hello."

There was a chorus of greetings as Mum held the phone up behind her. She was in the clubhouse, and it was packed. "All right, shut it now," she called. "They wanted to say hello and to tell you we miss you."

My heart ached. God, I loved my family. "Thank you. I love you all," I called loudly.

We chatted for a little while before Mum handed the phone over to Dad.

"Kid" was all he said with a smile. Having me gone was still hitting him hard. It'd only been a few weeks, though, so it was understandable since I still missed them like a toddler without a comfort blanket too.

"They treatin' you well?"

"Yeah, Dad. They are. I'd be a mess and homesick if it wasn't for Eve and Quake."

"Better stay that way."

I smiled. "Miss you, old man."

"Miss you, kid. Love you."

"Love you always."

"I'll let you get back to work. Text or call for anything."

"Wait," I called and then I asked him about the job I was

working on for Loyal, and he talked me through some things, which always helped both of us.

HOURS LATER, my alarm sounded through my headphones. I removed them and turned off the alarm before smiling over at the brothers painting the far wall. "Hey, I've got to go. Anyone need anything?"

"We're good, kid," Boomer said.

"Cool, cool," I said as I slipped out of my coveralls. I washed my hands and grabbed my keys. "Later," I called.

Out at my bike, which I'd shipped over—and cost me an arm and a leg—I straddled the seat and waited.

The door to the compound opened to reveal Eve and Quake. Seeing them made me all mushy on the inside. I hoped that feeling never went away. Quake said something that made Eve grin wide.

I loved watching them.

My loves.

My future.

If I had a dick, I'd walk around with a constant lady boner for those two.

"Hey, little devil," Quake said before he planted a kiss on my lips. "What are you thinkin' about with that cheeky smile?"

"Lady boners," I answered honestly, which made them laugh.

Eve replaced Quake and gave me a sweet, gentle peck. "Hey, babe," I said softly.

"How's your day been?" she asked.

"Good. You?"

"I was helping Dusty in the kitchen. Trying to hide all the new treats from a certain mammoth of a man."

"Ha." I faced Quake as he got on his ride and Eve made her way over to him. "Tell me you found all the hidden spots and we're gonna eat great things later?"

He winked. "Of fuckin' course."

Before I put my helmet on, I asked, "So where are we going?"

Eve shrugged from where she sat behind Quake. Our man grinned. "You'll see." He pushed his helmet on, as did Eve, and started his baby.

I quickly did the same. The roar of the engine revved, and I couldn't contain my laugh. Eve and Quake smiled over at me before Quake kicked up his stand and rode off. I followed, the front gate already sliding open.

It was lucky I hadn't taken on any clients outside of the clubhouse as they wouldn't be able to get in. The brothers and their families kept me booked up anyway, which was freaking wicked.

Quake pulled out onto the road, and we made it just down the street when he rode into a driveway.

Did he forget something?

But he was shutting his bike down and telling Eve to get off the back. I parked and did the same. When I got my helmet off, I asked, "Everything okay? Did you forget something? Might be faster if we rode back and went in to grab it instead of parking in someone's driveway. What happens if they get home?"

"They won't," Quake said.

Eve huffed. "How do you know that?"

"Because we own it."

Say what now?

"Huh?"

"Wait, what?" Eve said.

"Thought it'd be good to have our own place. Somewhere we can settle, and it's close to the compound. But that's if you both like it. There's a cooling-off period, so we've got time if it's not what you two pictured."

There was a frantic, excited rush to my pulse.

Eve hugged her helmet to her chest. "Hang on. You... bought this house?"

It was a cute brick home with a two-car garage connected to the side. The front looked absolutely adorable.

I wanted to see inside.

Quake nodded. He cleared his throat. "Yeah. It's got three bedrooms, a living room, and a family room, an office, two bathrooms, laundry, kitchen, and dining area. It's outdated so needs some work done on the inside, but it's something we can fix up together."

"You bought a house for us?" Eve whispered, tears forming.

"If you both like it," he said again with a cute blush.

I placed my helmet on my seat and skipped over to Eve with a big smile. I took her helmet and put it down before I grabbed her hand and pulled her over to Quake.

"There aren't enough words to describe how you and Eve make me feel. I love you with every inch of my body.

What you've done.... It's.... Holy shit, I can't.... It means so, so much, Kayson. You're seeing what I've always seen: a future between the three of us that is real and amazing, and our ties are growing each and every day and..." I bounced on my feet, clutching Eve's hand who was grinning and crying. "I can't wait to start this next adventure with you both."

"It's a good thing then?" Quake asked, needing to confirm it. He shot a worried glance at Eve.

Eve reached out for his hand. "It's the best. You amaze me with how sweet and kind and wonderful you are, Kayson," she told him.

I yanked her into him, and we crushed each other in a three-way hug.

When I pulled back, I let out an excited shout and pumped my fist in the air. "Let's go see our house!"

Quake's happiness shone through his gaze and grin.

"But we have to come up with a way where I can pay—"

"No," Quake clipped, cutting me off.

I glared despite my wide grin. "Don't you no me."

Eve curled an arm around my shoulders as we followed Quake to the front door. "Don't worry. We can work together to get what we want."

Laughing, I leaned into her and kissed her neck. "So true, and usually we don't have to work too hard."

Quake groaned. "Fuck me. We'll talk."

We pushed up behind him, hugging his back as he unlocked the door to our future.

ACKNOWLEDGMENTS

Coming back to the Hawks MC is always like coming home. I can't believe this series is still going. It wouldn't be if it wasn't for my amazing readers who keep these characters thriving, so thank you for your continued love for the Hawks MC. Coming in (fingers crossed) 2026 will be Aeila's story—Julian and Mattie's daughter or Rayne's—Stoke and Malinda's daughter.

A forever and massive thank-you must go to my wonderful editor, Becky, at Hot Tree Editing. I'm so glad we made that deal: you can never leave me now (insert evil laugh).

Big thanks also go to my daughter, Shayla, my alpha readers Lindsey Lawson and Maggie Savarese, and my beta readers, Amanda Evans, Amanda Berry, MJ Book Obsessed, and A. Trev.

I also wanted to give a shout out to these awesome book bloggers:
Danish Book Queen:
https://www.instagram.com/danishbookqueen/
The Dragons Den Book Blog:

https://www.instagram.com/bookblog_the_dragon_
den/

Book Hunter Yesse:

https://www.instagram.com/book.hunter.yesse/

Jaymie, Girlogic Reads:

https://www.instagram.com/girlogicreads/

Evleen, ReadsWithEv:

https://www.instagram.com/readswithev/

Christine, Just a Girl Cherry Pickin:

https://www.instagram.com/justagirlcherrypickin/

ALSO BY LILA ROSE

Hawks MC: Ballarat Charter

Holding Out: Zara and Talon

Outplayed: Violet and Travis

Climbing Out: Griz and Deanna

Finding Out (novella) Killer and Ivy

Black Out: Blue and Clary

No Way Out: Stoke and Malinda

Coming Out (novella) Julian and Mattie

Out to Find Freedom: Warden and Emmy

Hawks MC: Caroline Springs Charter

The Secrets Out: Josie, Pick, and Billy

Hiding Out: Dodge and Low

Down and Out: Dive and Mena

Living Without: Vicious and Nary

Walkout (novella) Dallas and Melissa

Hear Me Out: Beast and Knife

Break Out (novella) Handle and Della

Fallout: Fang and Poppy

Out of the Blue: Lan, Parker, and Easton

Out Gamed: Nancy and Gamer

Hawks MC: Next Generation

Coyote

Ruin

Texas

Swan

Romania

Diamond MC

Country

State (novella)

Death

Torch

Polished P & P

(MM romances)

Wreck Me Forever

Never A Saint

Working Out West

Up in a Blaze

Romantic Comedies

Fumbled Love

Bumbled Love

Making Changes

Making Sense

Why choose fantasy titles under L. Rose

A Torn Paige

A Lost Paige

A Final Paige

Within the Darkness

Infinite Bond

Protected by the Shifters series

(MM romances)

Protected by the Bear Shifter

Protected by the Tiger Shifter

Protected by the Fox Shifter